CIRCUS DAYS AGAIN

CIRCUS DAYS AGAIN

Enid Blyton

First published in the U.K. by
George Newnes Ltd. First published in this edition in 1972 by
William Collins Sons & Co. Ltd.,
14 St. James's Place, London S.W.1.

© Enid Blyton 1942

Printed in Great Britain by
Love & Malcomson Ltd.,
Brighton Road, Redhill, Surrey.

THE CIRCUS IS ON THE ROAD

LUMBERING down the dusty lanes one warm May day went a strange procession. The country-folk stared in surprise, and stopped their work to watch it pass.

"It's a circus!" said one to another. "Look—there's an elephant! And there's a funny creature—a chimpanzee, isn't he?"

It *was* a circus! It was Mr. Galliano's famous circus, on its way to its next show-place. With it was the circus-boy, Jimmy, and his famous dog, Lucky. Lotta the circus-girl was there, riding on her lovely pony, Black Beauty. Mr. Wally was in his car with Sammy, his clever chimpanzee. Sammy was dressed properly, in coat and trousers, and he kept raising his hat most politely to all the country-folk he passed. How they laughed to see him!

Lilliput, with his four monkeys, passed by. Jemina, his favourite little monkey, was curled as usual about his neck, her tiny teeth lovingly nibbling his left ear. She waved a small paw as she passed the wondering country-folk.

The glorious circus-horses trotted by, their proud heads held up well, their coats shining like satin. With them were Lotta's mother and father, Lal and Laddo. In a big travelling-cage behind came their performing dogs, yapping a little because of the heat of the day.

Mr. Volla was in a big cage with his five clumsy bears. They were not very fond of going from place to place, and he liked to be with them to quiet them. Dobby, his favourite bear, sat with his arm round his trainer, grunting a little when the cage jolted over a rut. The side-doors were open because of the warm weather, and the bears could see all that they passed. They liked that.

Sticky Stanley, the clown, got all the laughs as usual,

when he walked upside down on his hands, or gambolled about, making the silliest jokes. Every one loved old Sticky Stanley, and no matter where he was, he was always the same, merry, comical, and friendly. Oona, the acrobat, sat in his caravan watching Sticky Stanley. He was too lazy to join him just then.

The caravans and cages and horses went slowly by. There was no hurry. The circus was not opening until two nights ahead, and Mr. Galliano was hoping that the marvellous weather would hold out so that the circus would take a great deal of money.

"Then," thought the ring-master, tipping his hat so much to one side that it nearly fell off, "then I shall make my circus bigger! I shall get more clowns. I shall get more performing animals. My circus will be more famous than ever!"

A pretty yellow caravan went by. It had blue wheels and a blue chimney. It belonged to Mrs. Brown, Jimmy's mother. Jimmy, his mother, and Brownie, his father, all lived in the pretty caravan together. Jimmy had bought it for his mother with the money that he and his clever dog, Lucky, had earned in the circus-ring.

It was a fine caravan. It had taps to turn on over a little sink—and this was something that not even Mr. Galliano's caravan had! It had four bunks that folded flat against the wall. Jimmy slept in one and loved it. It had a fine cooking-stove, and gay curtains that flapped in and out of the windows in the little breeze. Mrs. Brown was very proud of her caravan.

She was cooking something on the stove. The smoke went up the chimney and floated away on the hot May air. Jimmy smelt his dinner cooking and went to find out what it was. Lucky came with him, running happily on four springy paws. She was a beautiful fox-terrier, smooth-haired, small, with a half-black, half-sandy head. Her eyes were soft and brown, and she loved Jimmy better than anyone else in the world.

Next to Jimmy she loved Lotta, the circus-girl—but if she had to choose between being with Lotta or being with Jimmy, it was always Jimmy she chose! Like a shadow

6

she kept at the boy's heels, and every night slept at his feet in the bunk.

Lucky was a valuable dog. She was one of the cleverest dogs that Mr. Galliano had ever seen, and it was Jimmy who had trained her. The little dog could do the most marvellous tricks, and went into the circus-ring every night with Jimmy. Lotta went too, with her beautiful black pony, which Lucky could ride almost as well as the two children could! It was funny to see the small dog balancing herself cleverly on Black Beauty's back, bumping up and down as the horse went round the ring!

"Mother, isn't it hot!" cried Jimmy, as he jumped up the steps at the back of the caravan. "What's for dinner? It's a lovely smell."

"Oh, Jimmy, surely you can't eat any dinner after eating four sausages for breakfast!" laughed his mother. "I've got Irish stew here."

"Can Lotta come and share it?" asked Jimmy eagerly. "She's only got ham sandwiches, and she says they'll be very dry!"

Lotta's mother, Lal, was not the good cook that Mrs. Brown was, and Lotta loved to come and share the delicious meals that Jimmy's mother prepared. Mrs. Brown was fond of the little girl, so she nodded her head.

"Yes. Call her. She loves Irish stew." Jimmy shouted for Lotta and she came running, her curly hair flying in the wind.

"Irish stew! Come and have some!" yelled Jimmy. Lotta was up the caravan steps with a bound. Mrs. Brown turned and looked at her.

"What a dirty little grub you are!" she said. "After all the trouble I've taken in teaching you how to be clean and tidy too. If you want any stew, go and wash your hands and do your hair. And how in the world did you manage to get that frock so dirty? Have you been sweeping a chimney or something?"

Lotta grinned and made a face. She went to turn the tap on at Mrs. Brown's neat sink.

"Oh no, Lotta! You just go and wash in your own caravan in the pail there," cried Mrs. Brown. "You're so dirty you'll make my nice clean sink black. Go along with you."

It wasn't any use arguing with Mrs. Brown, as Lotta knew. So down the steps she went again and flew to her own caravan, which was not nearly so pretty or so clean as Jimmy's. She rinsed her hands in the pail of water there, ran a wet towel over her face, brushed her flying curls, and tied a ribbon on one side. She looked to see if she had a clean dress, but each one seemed even blacker than the one she had on, so she gave that up as a bad job.

Only Lotta's beautiful, spangled circus-frock was clean and fresh. However untidy and dirty the circus-folk looked in their everyday clothes, they kept their ring-suits and frocks very carefully indeed. The tiniest tear was always mended. The smallest spot was washed out. Nothing must spoil them when they were worn in the ring.

The two children talked about the next show-place as they ate their stew. The town they were going to was a big one.

"Mr. Galliano plans to have a bigger circus if we do well at Bigminton," said Jimmy. "Won't that be fun, Lotta?"

"What will he have if it's to be bigger?" asked Lotta.

"He might have another elephant—or a sea-lion. Sea-lions are marvellous at performing tricks," said Jimmy. "I'm almost sure he's going to have more clowns. One clown isn't nearly enough really, though Sticky Stanley is simply marvellous."

"Well, he can't have any more horses or dogs because we've plenty of those," said Lotta, holding out her plate for some more stew. "Won't it be lovely to have more people in the circus. I hope they'll be nice."

The circus procession rumbled on as the children ate their dinner. The sun shone through the windows of the blue caravan. Old Jumbo, the elephant in front, trumpeted because he wanted a drink. The dogs in the travelling-cages yelped too. They wanted a run.

"Listen to them," said Lotta. "I hope we get to our camping-place soon. They do so want to stretch their legs. Shall we take them for a walk, Jimmy, when we camp for the night?"

8

So, when the sun was sinking, and the circus arranged itself around a big field, the two children slipped open the door of the dogs' big cage, and let them all out.

"Punch! Judy! Pincher! Toby! Come on, all of you!" cried Lotta. "Lucky, hie, Lucky, you come too. And where's Lulu the spaniel, Jimmy? Oh, there she is! Come, Lulu—we're all off for a run."

The camp settled in whilst the children took the restless dogs for a run. Jumbo was tied to a big tree. He caressed his keeper, Mr. Tonks, with his trunk, glad to be able to take a rest. Mr. Tonks spoke softly to the big animal. They were the best friends in the world.

Sammy the chimpanzee sat down to a meal with Mr. Wally, his master. Mr. Wally talked to him as if he could understand every word—and really, it seemed as if Sammy could, for he jabbered back at Mr. Wally as if he were really answering him.

The little monkey-man, Lilliput, set a tub upside down, and put some oranges and bananas on it for his four monkeys. They sat round it, peeling their bananas and chattering. Jemina peeled a large banana, bit it in half, and offered the other half to Lilliput. When another monkey snatched it from her, she flew at him and pulled off the little coat he was wearing.

"Now, now, Jemina!" said Lilliput, peeling a banana quickly. "Look—I'll bite this in half—and *you* shall have the other half. There."

Jemima was pleased. She took the half-banana and ate it quickly, chattering with pleasure. Then, quick as lightning, she stuffed the peel down the neck of the other monkey. Squealing with merriment she leapt away to the top of her master's caravan. She held on to the chimney and watched the other monkey trying to get the peel from the neck of his little red coat.

The horses whinnied as Lal and Laddo rubbed them down. The five bears grunted as they ate their evening meal. Mr. Volla gave them each a large piece of toffee afterwards, and it was funny to watch the bears solemnly sucking it, enjoying the sweetness.

Lotta and Jimmy came back with all the dogs, happy

now after a long run. The children saw them safely into their cage, all except Lulu and Lucky, and then went to get some cocoa and biscuits from Mrs. Brown.

The camp had settled in. The camp-fires burned like glow-worms in the dark field. Sticky Stanley got out his guitar and sang a funny little song. But the circus-folk were too tired to gather round and listen that night. One by one they went to their caravans and fell asleep.

"Isn't it fun to belong to a travelling circus!" said Jimmy sleepily to little dog Lucky, as he climbed into his bunk. "We'll have some fun here, Lucky. Good-night—and don't nibble my toes till the morning."

MADAME PRUNELLA AND
HER PARROTS

THE circus opened at Bigminton after a day or two's rest. The weather kept fine, and Mr. Galliano was delighted to see so many people paying their money at the gate.

"You shall have a new dress," he promised Lotta, sticking his hat on one side. "And you, Jimmy, shall have a new ring-suit that shines like the moon."

All the circus-folk liked to wear the loveliest suits and dresses that they could possibly afford, when they appeared in the ring. The shinier the better. Lotta longed to have a dress so covered with spangles that the dress itself could hardly be seen. Jimmy didn't mind so much, though he too liked to feel grand when he went into the ring. But how he loved to dress up little dog Lucky.

Lucky had quite a wardrobe of coats and collars and bows. Jimmy's mother kept them all clean and mended, and laughed to see Lucky parading up and down in a grand new coat or stiff bow.

"You and Jemima the monkey and Sammy the chimpanzee are all as vain as little girls," she said. "As for Jemima, I wonder she doesn't carry a looking-glass about with her to see if her whiskers are straight."

Oona the acrobat came by and called to Jimmy. "Hie, there! Would you like to come with me and visit my cousin? She lives near here, and maybe she's going to join the circus."

"Oooh, yes!" said Jimmy, and jumped down the steps with Lucky at his heels. "Where's Lotta? She'd like to come too."

Lotta was practising in the ring. She had Black Beauty there, and was galloping round and round, standing lightly

11

on his back. When her father shouted "Hup!" she jumped right round and stood facing the horse's tail. When he shouted again she leapt round the other way. It was marvellous to watch her.

"Lotta! Have you nearly finished?" cried Jimmy. "Oona's going to visit his cousin, and I'm going with him."

"I'll come too," said Lotta, and she leapt lightly off the horse's back. She turned to her father. "Can I go now, Laddo?" she asked. She called her mother Lal and her father Laddo, as everyone else did.

"Yes, you can go," said Laddo. "Leave Black Beauty. I want to trot him round with the other horses. He's a great help to them, he's so clever."

Lotta and Jimmy ran off with Oona. They asked him about his cousin. "Who is she? What does she do? Is she an animal-trainer?"

Oona laughed. "Well—not exactly an *animal*-trainer. She keeps parrots."

"Parrots!" squealed Lotta. "Oh, I love parrots! What do hers do? Do they talk? Does she take them into the ring?"

"Of course," said Oona. "They talk, they recite—and they sing a song together. One of them, I forget its name, is very clever indeed. It can hold a brush in its claws and brush its crest. It can do a little dance too, whilst the music plays and the others sing."

"Golly!" said Jimmy. "That will be fun. I've never had anything to do with birds before. I wonder if they'll like me as much as the animals do."

Oona looked at Jimmy and laughed. "Oh, you'll find that all Madame Prunella's parrots will let you do what you like with them," he said. "You've got the secret of handling every live creature there is, Jimmy—and the parrots will be all over you."

They caught a tram and went down into the heart of Bigminton. They came to a ramshackle little house, with a notice in the window, "Rooms to let." As they knocked at the door a chorus of screeches rose on the air from inside the house.

Then a deep voice spoke: "Come in, wipe your feet, shut the door, and say how-do-you-do."

Jimmy looked astonished. This was a funny greeting, he thought. He wasn't sure if he was going to like Madame Prunella if she spoke to them like this. Lotta saw his face and laughed.

"That's not your cousin speaking, is it?" she cried to Oona. "It's one of the parrots, isn't it?"

"Of course," said Oona, and he opened the door. Another voice called out in a sing-song manner:

"Here comes the sweep! Swee-ee-eep! Swee-ee-eeep! Wash your face, my dear, wash your face."

The children laughed. That was another parrot, they knew. What fun! They all went into a tiny room, and Oona kissed a small, fat little woman there. She was in a dressing-gown, sewing, and around her were about a dozen parrots, some grey and red, some the most brilliant colours imaginable.

"Good morning," she said. "Excuse me getting up, but I've lost my shoes this morning, and there are pins everywhere. I upset the pin-box, you see—and now I daren't leave my chair to look for my shoes in case I prick my feet."

The children looked at the small, fat-cheeked little woman and liked her very much. Her eyes were small, and almost buried in her plump cheeks, but they shone and twinkled like blue beads. Her head was a mass of tight black curls. One parrot sat on her shoulder, singing a soft little song, and the others talked and screeched around. It was rather like being in the parrot-house at the Zoo. Every one had to shout, for they couldn't be heard unless they did.

"This is Lotta, and this is Jimmy," cried Oona to his cousin.

"Oh, I've heard of Jimmy and his wonderful dog, Lucky," said Madame Prunella, smiling. "Where is she?"

"I left her with my mother," said Jimmy. "I don't much like bringing her among a lot of traffic. You'll see her if you join Mr. Galliano's circus. I do hope you *do*, Madame

Prunella. I'd love to get to know some birds. I've only had animals so far."

"My parrots will never go to anyone but to me," said Madame Prunella proudly. "I have trained them all myself, and look after them myself—and not one will allow itself to be handled by a stranger."

As she spoke, a large red-and-grey parrot lifted its crest up very high, and spoke in a deep voice. "Eggs and bacon, ham and cheese, coffee and biscuits!" it remarked, and then, very solemnly, hopped along the edge of the bookcase where it was perched, and rubbed its great curved beak against Jimmy's cheek.

Madame Prunella stared in the greatest surprise. "Look at Gringle!" she cried. "Gringle! You are making love to Jimmy! You have never done that to anyone before! What's happened to you?"

"Ham and tongue, tomatoes and eggs, toffee and chocolate," said the parrot, and stepped straight on to Jimmy's left shoulder!

Then it opened its beak and gave such a terrific screech that made Lotta jump, and gave Jimmy such a fright that he rushed to the other side of the room! The parrot flew off his shoulder, sat on the top of the curtain, and laughed like a naughty boy who had played a joke.

Every one else laughed too. "Oh, Jimmy! You did look scared!" said Lotta.

"I should think so," said Jimmy indignantly. "Screaming like an express train right in my ear."

"Mushrooms and kippers," remarked the parrot, scratching its head.

"That parrot seems to think of nothing but food," said Jimmy.

Madame Prunella stared at Jimmy. "Gringle has never behaved like that before," she said. "Jimmy, go round the other parrots and see if they will rub their heads against you, or talk. Mind that green-and-red one over there—he's a bit bad-tempered and may tear your hand with his beak. Go slowly."

Jimmy was only too pleased to go round the parrots. Lotta watched proudly. She knew better than anyone how marvellous Jimmy was with all live creatures. She had watched him with fierce tigers! She had seen him with bears and monkeys. She knew how dogs and horses all loved him. She knew that the parrots would make friends with him at once.

And so they did. As soon as the big birds knew that Jimmy wanted to be friendly, they crowded round him, muttering, screeching, talking. Two perched on his shoulders. One tried to sit on his head. The others flew round him, making quite a wind with their big wings.

Jimmy laughed. "I like them," he said. "They are clever birds, Madame Prunella. Oh, do come and join our circus, and let me help you with your parrots. I'd love to know them."

"Well, I *was* thinking of joining Mr. Phillippino's Circus," said Madame Prunella, "but as my cousin is with Mr. Galliano's, and *you* are there, Jimmy, I'll come! I'd like to see you handling my parrots. Maybe you could teach them some new tricks."

Jimmy beamed. It would be fun to have plump-cheeked little Madame Prunella in the circus. She looked such a comical, good-tempered little person.

But suddenly he had another glimpse of her—one that surprised him and Lotta very much. She jumped up from her chair to take one of her parrots—and trod on one of the pins that lay all about the floor. She gave a screech just like one of her parrots, held her foot and danced angrily about, treading on yet more pins with her other foot!

Madame Prunella was in a temper—and *such* a temper! She screeched, she shouted, she yelled—and all the parrots with one accord flew as far away from her as they could! She caught hold of the table-cloth and flapped it wildly. She picked up a broom and ran at the two children as if she would sweep them from the room. They were quite frightened.

"Come away," said Oona, grinning. "Prunella is in one of her tantrums. She'll get out of it as quickly as she got into it—but it's safer to go when she's like this!"

The children fled down the little path to the gate. They could hear the shouting and screeching of the parrots behind them. Gringle was yelling, "Pepper and mustard, pepper and mustard!" at the top of his voice.

"Golly! Pepper and mustard is just about right when Madame Prunella loses her temper!" said Jimmy. "What a funny person! I like her, though she gets into tantrums—and I do like the parrots. I hope she joins the circus and comes along with us."

A curtain was pulled aside and a window was thrown open. Madame Prunella looked out, smiling.

"Tell Galliano I'll come along to-morrow," she called. "About twelve o'clock!"

Like an April shower Madame Prunella's temper had passed away. Gringle was on her shoulder, rubbing against her ear. "Sugar and spice," he said. "Sugar and spice."

"We shall have some fun with Madame Prunella!" said Oona, grinning. And he was right!

MADAME PRUNELLA JOINS THE SHOW

JIMMY and Lotta told Mrs. Brown all about Madame Prunella and her parrots and tantrums. Mrs. Brown was amused.

"Well, if parrots join this circus, there will be even more chattering!" she said, smiling at the children, who had both been talking at once. "Jimmy, Lal has been shouting for you. He wants you to go and see to the dogs."

It was part of Jimmy's work to help with the performing dogs, and he loved this. Every dog adored Jimmy and when he came near their cage they all pressed against the wire, some standing up on their hind-legs to go near to him. Lucky, his own dog, ran at his heels, for Jimmy would never allow her to be shut up in a cage, valuable though she was.

"I say, Jimmy, it would be rather fun to tease Madame Prunella and get her into a few tempers, wouldn't it?" said Lotta. "I do think she was funny, don't you?"

"Yes," said Jimmy, washing out all the dog's dishes. "We'll have a good time with her. I like her. Here, Lotta, dry these dishes. Surely you can do a bit of work too?"

"I've done my work this morning," said Lotta lazily. "I've groomed Black Beauty, and exercised him, and done my practice in the tent. This is your work, not mine."

Jimmy took hold of her tiny pink ear and led her to where a clean cloth was hanging. "I shan't stand any nonsense from *you*!" he said. "I'll go to Mr. Galliano and tell him I won't let you share my turn to-night in the ring!"

Lotta wriggled away, grinning. She and Jimmy were

very good friends, though they often teased one another. She began to dry the dishes.

"Isn't it windy up here?" she said. "You know, we're not very far from the sea, Jimmy. We might go down and bathe one afternoon."

"I can smell the sea in the wind," said Jimmy, sniffing. "I hope the breeze doesn't get any stronger. The tents are flapping enough already!"

Jemima the monkey sidled by. She snatched Lotta's drying-cloth and tore off with it. Lotta gave a squeal of rage and ran after her. The tiny monkey was a ball of mischief, and loved to tease Lotta. She jumped up on to the top of Jimmy's caravan, and twisted the cloth round the smoking chimney.

"You wait till I get you!" cried Lotta. The monkey leapt off the caravan roof and shot up a tree, where she sat grinning and chattering, looking down at the two children. The cloth waved wildly from the chimney, much to Mrs. Brown's amazement when she came in from doing a bit of shopping, and there it stayed till Jimmy climbed up and fetched it down, black and smoky.

The circus opened well. Mr. Wally and his wonderful chimpanzee, Sammy, amazed every one, and they had to come back half a dozen times after their turn and bow all around the ring. Sammy loved the clapping and the cheering. He took off his hat and waved it wildly, which made every one cheer all the more.

The horses and their beautiful dancing were always loved by every one. Lal and Laddo looked magnificent in their circus-suits as the rode their horses, glittering and shining, under the flaring circus-lights. The dogs, too, were cheered, and indeed they were very clever in the way they walked, jumped, played ball, carried flags, and did all kinds of tricks. Lal and Laddo patted them and rewarded them with kind words and biscuits, and the happy little dogs wagged their tails like leaves waving in the wind!

Lotta and Jimmy, who were known as the two Wonder-Children, always got long and loud cheers and claps, for little dog Lucky, and the pony Black Beauty, were marvellous in their tricks. When Lucky leapt on to Black

18

Beauty's back just as Lotta had done, the cheers almost brought the roof down! It was great fun, and both children and animals loved it.

The children had to go to bed very late when the circus was on, but they were used to this. Mrs. Brown saw that Jimmy went straight to bed, instead of chattering and laughing with the other circus-folk after the show, and she had told Lal, Lotta's mother, that she would see to the little girl too.

"Thanks," said Lal. "I have to see to the horses and dogs with Laddo—so if you *will* see that Lotta is safe in bed, instead of rushing round till midnight, I'd be grateful! "

Madame Prunella did not join the circus for a few days. She sent word to say that one of her parrots was ill, but she would come before the week-end. The children were delighted. They hung on the field-gate about the time that Madame Prunella was expected—and at last they saw her caravan arriving. It was a very gay one indeed!

It was bright orange, with blue wheels, and the horse that pulled it had his mane plaited with blue and orange ribbons, and his tail plaited too. He was an old circus-horse, and his delight at sniffing the old smells of the ring was sweet to see. He whinnied to the other horses, and they whinnied back.

"What talks they'll have about old times! " said Jimmy, as he unharnessed Madame Prunella's horse and led him to where the other horses were. "There you are, old boy —have a good feed, and a chat about all the circuses you have ever been in! "

Madame Prunella was standing the perches of her parrots outside in the sun. Each parrot was chained by the leg to its perch, and they all screeched and squealed at the tops of their voices. Madame Prunella scratched them on their heads, and they chattered away happily.

"Kippers and herrings," said Gringle solemnly to Jimmy. "Kippers and herrings."

"Pickles and sauce," answered Jimmy in just as solemn a voice. Gringle put out a foot and Jimmy shook hands with him.

"Gringle has certainly made friends with you," said

19

Madame Prunella. "But just you mind what I say, children —no playing about with my parrots, please, or I shall have something to say to you!"

Jemima the monkey came near and the parrots set up a great screeching. Jemima grinned and chattered back. She took off her little hat and put it on a parrot's head. The parrot took it off in anger and threw it on the ground.

"'You'd better tell Jemima, too, not to play about with the parrots!" grinned Jimmy. "I say, what a row they make! I can see my mother getting headaches all the day long! I'd better move our caravan a bit farther off!"

"Boy, my parrots can be as quiet as mice in a corner!" said Madame Prunella with a gleam in her eye. She swung round on her brilliant birds. "Hush!" she said. "Hush! The baby is asleep!"

At once every parrot was quiet. The children looked about for the baby. They couldn't see one anywhere.

"There just isn't a real baby," said Madame Prunella. "It's just one of our circus tricks. Whenever I say the word 'baby' they have to be quiet."

The parrot-woman had a very untidy caravan. It smelt of parrots, and it really seemed as if there was no room for anything else but a bed for her and a stove inside the caravan. All the rest of the room was taken up by cages or perches. Prunella loved her parrots so much that, like Mr. Wally and his chimpanzee, she would not be parted from her pets even at night. Jimmy had often seen Sammy the chimp sleeping peacefully in his bunk opposite to Mr. Wally in his caravan. He couldn't imagine how Madame Prunella could bear to sleep with twelve parrots!

"Still, I wouldn't let Lucky sleep anywhere but with me," he thought. "So I suppose if Madame Prunella loves her parrots as I love dogs, she feels the same."

Madame Prunella took her parrots into the ring that night. They were an enormous success! Jimmy could hardly believe his ears at the things they could say and sing.

They all knew the nursery rhymes, of course, and they could all count and say the alphabet. Gringle could reel off the names of all kinds of food, and Pola, another grey-and-red parrot, could recite long poems. When they sang together it was very funny indeed, for although they knew the words well, they did not always keep good time, and the band, which played the music for them, had to keep going slowly or quickly to keep time to the parrots' loud, harsh voices!

Gringle could whistle too—and his cleverest trick of all was his imitation of all kinds of noises!

"Now, Gringle, tell us how an aeroplane goes," said Madame Prunella, who was very plump and pretty in a brilliant blue-and-gold skirt and bodice, with golden feathers nodding in her hair.

Gringle swelled out his throat and opened his beak —and from it there came the throbbing sound of an aeroplane! It was really marvellous.

"And now I want an ice, Gringle," said Madame Prunella. "Where's the ice-cream man?"

The sound of an ice-cream man's bell came jingling into the ring. Jimmy looked round in surprise—surely the ice-cream man would not be allowed in the ring! But it was only Gringle, making the exact noise of the tricycle bell!

"Now it's firework night! The fireworks are going off, Gringle!" cried Prunella—and from the clever parrot came the noises of pops and explosions, splutters and bangs—for all the world like fireworks going off on Guy Fawkes' Day! It was really most extraordinary.

Gringle could cry like a baby, howl like a wolf, and mew like a cat. Jimmy and Lotta thought he must be the cleverest parrot in the whole world.

When the people cheered and yelled and clapped, the parrots went mad with joy. They danced from side to side on their perches, and screeched loudly above the applause.

"Sh! The baby's asleep!" said Prunella, and at once every parrot was quiet. They each bowed solemnly round the ring and then, fluttering round Madame Prunella, they were taken from the ring.

"Madame Prunella, we are proud to have you here," said Mr. Galliano, delighted, his hat well on one side. "Your turn is good, very good, yes. We shall do well at Bigminton!"

And so they did! The money poured in, and Mr. Galliano went whistling round the circus-camp, paying every one well, and telling them that they were to stay another week in the windy, cliff-side camp. The children were pleased. They had discovered a short way to the beach and had bathed and paddled every afternoon.

"It's fine here!" said Jimmy. "I hope we have another good week, Lotta. I don't see why we shouldn't!"

But the next week wasn't quite what anyone expected!

WHAT HAPPENED ON
A WINDY NIGHT

THE second week opened well. The weather was not so good, and the wind blew even more strongly, but this did not seem to stop the Bigminton people from flocking to see Mr. Galliano's famous circus. Mr. Galliano bought himself a grand new circus-suit, which glittered so much that it almost dazzled Lotta to look at it. "Doesn't he look grand, standing in the middle of the ring, cracking his whip like that?" said Jimmy admiringly. "I'll be a circus-owner one day! I'll be a ring-master in top-hat and top-boots and a glittering suit, cracking a whip till it sounds like a pistol-shot!"

"I wish this wind would stop," said Lotta, pulling her coat closely round her shoulders. "It's so cold when it blows. The animals don't like it either."

Jimmy had noticed that often with the animals. They were restless and uneasy when the wind blew strongly. There were strange noises that the wind made, rattles and bangs, jiggles and whistlings, which made the animals constantly prick up their ears and turn this way and that.

The horses whinnied and stamped when the wind roared round the field. The dogs whined and growled. The monkeys sat shivering close together in Lilliput's caravan. They felt cold and frightened. Even Jumbo the elephant flapped his big ears in annoyance when the gale shrieked round his enormous head.

Lucky didn't mind the wind. She didn't mind anything so long as she was with Jimmy. But Black Beauty the pony looked round him with startled eyes when the wind flapped at his tail and sent a piece of paper rustling against

JUMBO THE ELEPHANT FLIPPED HIS BIG EARS IN ANNOYANCE

his beautiful legs. He whinnied for Lotta, and she went to soothe him and comfort him.

"It's only the wind," she told him. "Don't be afraid, Black Beauty. See how it blows my curls—*I* don't mind it! See how it flaps at my dress! It's only the wind."

The last night of the circus came. The wind had risen to a gale, and all the animals were nervous and restless. Mr. Galliano wondered whether he should put off the last night, but it was difficult to put posters up in the town to tell the people. The circus must open and do its best!

A great many people came, and soon the big top, as the great ring-tent was called, was full. The ring was strewn with sawdust, and the band took their places. Outside the wind roared steadily, drowning even the band at times! All the circus-folk felt they would be glad when the performance was safely over, for the horses and dogs were nervous and disobedient! Sammy the chimpanzee was very difficult. Just before he was due to enter the ring, he went into a corner and took off all his clothes!

"Sammy! How tiresome you are!" cried Mr. Wally. "Jimmy, come and help me to dress him, quickly. He does so hate the wind. He did this once before in a storm."

Sammy was dressed, but he was so naughty that he had to miss his turn in the ring, and go on later. Even so, he gave a bad performance and Mr. Wally was quite ashamed of him. One of the chimpanzee's tricks was to ride a bicycle round the ring, waving his hat to say good-bye—and then to ride right out of the ring like that.

But he wouldn't ride out! He kept on and on riding round the ring, making queer noises! He threw his hat at Mr. Wally, and nearly knocked him over when his trainer went to get him off the bicycle! But at last Jimmy went to help, and between them they got the naughty chimpanzee safely out of the ring and into his cage!

The wind went on howling round and round the tent. The ropes that held down the tent creaked, and the canvas flapped and swayed. Once or twice Mr. Galliano looked uneasily at the canvas walls of the tent, and to Jimmy's surprise he cut short two or three of the turns, and would not let Lotta go into the ring at all. The little girl was very angry, but she did not dare to grumble in front of Mr. Galliano.

The ring-master's hat was on quite straight—a thing that only happened when he was worried. Lal and Laddo, Mr. Volla and Mr. Wally, looked worried too. It was not good to know that their animals were nervous and afraid. It is only when an animal is afraid that a trainer finds it hard to handle him.

Lucky ran round Jimmy's heels, keeping very close to him. She knew that people were worried. When Mr. Galliano brought the circus to an end, half-an-hour before its time, Lotta and Jimmy went to hold torches so that the departing people might see their way out of the wind-swept field.

And no sooner had they all gone than a surprising and alarming thing happened. The gale blew down the big tent, in which was the circus-ring!

SNAP! went the ropes—and with a great flapping and creaking the enormous tent, so carefully put up by Jimmy's father and the other men, was lifted right up from the ground!

Jumbo the elephant trumpeted in terror—but he was safely tethered by a hind leg to a great tree, and he could not run away. Mr. Tonks ran to him at once.

The horses were all safely in their travelling-stables, for Lal and Laddo would not leave them out in such a gale. The dogs, too, were safe in their cages, and the side-doors were safely closed. Sammy was with Mr. Wally in his caravan, drinking hot milk and eating a bunch of bananas.

But Mr. Volla and his five bears were walking together across the dark, wind-swept field to their cage when the great white tent rose into the air and flew flapping over the grass. The bears saw the big white thing coming and they were terrified. They couldn't imagine *what* it was! Mr. Volla knew it was only the tent, and he pulled quickly at the thick rope which guided the bears. The tent missed them and flapped away—but the bears howled in fright. Two of them, Dobby and Grizel, broke the rope that held them, and ran grunting across the field.

"Help! Help!" yelled Mr. Volla. "Two of my bears

have escaped. Jimmy! Brownie! Wally! Where are you! Take my bears so that I can run after the others."

Jimmy heard him yelling and at once he and Lucky ran to help Mr. Volla. Brownie, Jimmy's father, ran too, and soon they were leading three frightened bears to their cages, whilst poor Mr. Volla ran wildly about the field shouting for his beloved bear-cub, Dobby, and the bigger bear, Grizel.

The whole circus turned out to help. The hedges and banks and ditches were thoroughly searched, and torches flashed all about the cliff-side. Mr. Volla yelled the names of his bears at the top of his voice, but they did not appear.

And then another thing happened! The big tent flapped itself round the field—and then laid itself very carefully right over the top of Madame Prunella's caravan! She was safely inside with her parrots, with all the windows shut. Her parrots, scared of the gale, were screeching loudly, and she let them screech. Other people might not like her parrots' harsh voices, but to Madame Prunella they were as sweet as the sound of larks or nightingales!

Madame Prunella did not know that the tent had draped itself over her caravan. She could hear nothing but her parrots. The birds knew that something strange had happened, and they squealed and screeched all the more.

Nobody noticed what the tent had done. Jimmy's father, who was the carpenter and handy-man of the circus, noticed only that the tent had come to rest—and he quickly pegged it down where it was, meaning to see to it in the morning. He was thankful that it had not blown down when the people of Bigminton had been inside!

Nobody guessed that Prunella's caravan was hidden beneath the tent. It was quite dark, and only the big white bulge of the enormous tent could be seen dimly by the light of the torches. So there the tent was left, with Madame Prunella's caravan beneath it, till the morning.

Every one was worried about the bears. Mr. Galliano knew only too well what might happen to escaped circus-animals. They would be shot without a doubt. Jimmy knew that too. He remembered how once Sammy the chimpanzee

27

had escaped, and how he, Jimmy, had only just managed to find and save Sammy before he was killed.

He went to find Lotta. The little girl was with Black Beauty, who was trembling nervously at all the shouting and upset.

"Lotta," said Jimmy. "Will you come with me? I'm going to find Mr. Volla's bears. Lucky can trace them for me, I'm sure—and if we manage to get on their track soon, we could bring them back before they are captured and shot by some one who doesn't know they are only harmless cidcus-animals."

"They may be harmless in the circus, Jimmy," said Lotta, "but when they are away from us and frightened and lonely, they may not be so harmless! They might hurt some one! All right—I'll come. Just give me time to put Black Beauty safely into his stable."

She slipped away. Jimmy went to the bears' cage and took Lucky to Dobby's sleeping-straw.

"Smell it, Lucky, smell it," said Jimmy, pressing his dog's sharp nose down into the straw. "Then we'll follow! Where's that cub, Dobby?"

Lucky yelped joyously. She liked Dobby, the comical, clumsy bear-cub. Dobby and she very often played together, and although the bear was heavy and powerful, he was always very gentle with the small dog.

Lucky sniffed eagerly, and then Jimmy took her to where the bears had escaped. Lucky put her nose to the ground and then, with a yelp, tore across the field! She had found Dobby's trail!

"Hie, Lucky! Come back!" cried Jimmy, looking round for Lotta. "Let me put you on a lead! I can't see you or follow you if you go tearing off like that!"

Lucky came back. Lotta appeared, wearing a thick coat and scarf, for the wind was still strong and bitterly cold. She held out a woollen scarf to Jimmy.

"Come on," she said. "Your mother has told Galliano that she can't find you, and if Galliano roars for us, we'll have to go to him. Hurry, before we're missed!"

So through the dark, windy night the two children followed little dog Lucky. She was on a lead, and she pulled and strained at it, as her sharp, doggy nose smelt the strong scent of the smell left by Dobby and Grizel, the two escaped bears.

"I hope they haven't gone too far!" said Jimmy anxiously. "Goodness knows where they might be by morning!"

"Well—we'll be there, too!" said brave Lotta. "I'll walk all night if it means we can get the bears before anything happens!"

THE HUNT FOR THE BEARS

THE two children made their way through the dark windy night, guided by Lucky, who was pulling hard at her lead. The wind was still very strong indeed and blew the clouds to rags—but every now and again the moon shone out and the children could see where they were.

"I say, Lucky is taking us down to the seashore!" said Jimmy anxiously. "I hope to goodness the bears haven't gone there."

But they had, for Lucky was still following their scent. Nose to ground she smelt out the footsteps of the two bears and whined a little because she couldn't go as fast as she liked.

Down a steep, rocky cliff-path went the two children— and when the moon came out for a moment, Jimmy gave a cry, and pointed to the ground.

"Look!" he said. "Can you see the claw-marks of Dobby and Grizel? See how they dug their claws into the path to keep themselves from slipping!"

The children reached the shore. They looked around, wondering if they would see the bears anywhere. The moon swept out from the clouds at that moment, and they could see the track of foot-marks going over the sand.

"Come on! They've gone that way!" cried Jimmy, pleased. "Hurry, Lotta—we may find them round the corner of that cliff."

They followed the foot-prints eagerly and went right round the point of the rocky cliff. Lucky pulled at the lead again, and the children let her drag them where she wanted to go. They could not see the foot-marks when the moon was behind the clouds, but Lucky could always smell them.

They went on round the cliff. A great wave suddenly tore up the beach and splashed Jimmy from head to foot. He looked at the dark raging sea in alarm.

"I say, Lotta! I wonder if we ought to have come all the way round that rocky cliff. If the tide's coming in, we may not be able to get back."

"Gracious!" said Lotta, frightened. "What sillies we are. Of course the tide is coming in. Jimmy, what shall we do —go back, do you think? The sea comes right up to the cliff here, when the tide is in. We may be cut off unless we get round that corner again quickly."

The moon sailed out again, and the restless sea tossed beneath the silver light. Another great wave came swirling up the beach, and the children jumped up on to a rock to escape it. Jimmy looked back.

"We're cut off already," he said, in dismay. "Look— the tide is right round that rocky corner. We'd never get back. Our only chance is to climb the cliff here."

"But where have the bears gone?" asked Lotta, who had almost forgotten them in the worry of the moment.

"Goodness knows," groaned Jimmy. "Swept off their feet and drowned, I expect. And the same thing will happen to us and Lucky if we don't get up this cliff mighty quick. Come on, Lucky—hurry! Look out, Lotta, there's another enormous wave."

The children began to climb the rocky cliff at the back of the shore. It was slippery, and when the moon went in, it was hard to feel the best way to climb. It was slow work too, and all the time the tide came in a little more, splashing foamy fingers up the cliff, trying to catch their feet.

"I don't like the sea when it behaves like this," said Lotta, half crying. "I'm cold and wet and frightened. We were silly to come, Jimmy. We didn't think of the darkness and the wind."

"Well, the wind's dying down a bit now," said Jimmy, helping Lotta over a slippery piece of rock. "Come on— here's a nice easy bit now."

"Have we got to stay and shiver on this cliff all night long?" asked Lotta miserably, her teeth chattering. "My goodness—what will every one say?"

The wind certainly was dying down. It no longer wailed and roared around them like a mad thing. The clouds in the sky slowed down a little, and the moon shone more steadily.

"Look! There's a cave or something over there," said Jimmy suddenly. He had spied a dark opening just above them. "Let's see if we can get in there, Lotta. We shall at least be sheltered from the gale."

They waited for the moon to sail out once again and then they climbed up to the cave. The opening was small, but big enough to squeeze into. It was so dark inside that the children could see nothing at all. They groped their way in, and found a rocky ledge to sit on. It was quiet and sheltered there—but how cold the two children were!

"I think we've behaved very stupidly," said Lotta, shivering. "We just rushed off after the bears without thinking. Why in the world didn't we bring a torch? We shall both get awful colds too, sitting here all night—and then we shan't be able to go into the ring and Galliano will be angry and scold us for being stupid."

The two sat and thought about Mr. Galliano. He was very good-tempered when things went well, but both children had been in trouble before with him, and they knew that he might be angry about this. Whatever had made them come out without telling some one? Now no one would know where they were, and half the circus-folk would waste the night looking for them. Worst of all, nobody would find them in the little cave half-way up the dark cliff.

Lotta shivered so much that Jimmy was anxious about her. He lifted Lucky on to her knee.

"Cuddle her," he said. "She's warm, Lotta. I'd give you my coat only it's so wet. I wonder if there's any dry seaweed in the cave. I'll feel around and see. We could make a kind of bed of that."

He got up and began to stumble round the cave. It was quite big inside. Jimmy felt about but could find no seaweed —only sand on the floor and stones, and rock all around.

And then the two children suddenly heard a most peculiar noise in the cave. They listened. It sounded exactly like somebody breathing.

"Lotta! Can you hear that noise?" asked Jimmy, coming

back to her. "Do you think it's the wind—or the sound of the sea coming up into the cave?

"No," said Lotta, holding his hand rather tightly. "It's in the cave. But whatever can it be? It's funny that Lucky doesn't growl or bark. She always does if there's any stranger about, or if anything's wrong."

Lucky wagged her tail. She settled down even more comfortably on Lotta's knee. The breathing in the cave didn't seem to worry her at all.

The children listened hard. The noise went on and on, regularly, as if some one was fast asleep and breathing peacefully.

"Well, I'm going to see what is making that noise," said Jimmy, at last. "I can't sit here and wonder any more. If there's something in this cave I'm going to find out what it is. Here, Lucky—come with me."

"Be careful, Jimmy," said Lotta.

Jimmy and Lucky made their way to the back of the cave. Lucky didn't bark or growl at all. Jimmy couldn't understand it.

And then he suddenly touched something warm—and furry—and soft. He jumped in surprise.

A grunt came from the furry bundle at the back of the cave. Jimmy gave such a yell that Lotta fell off the ledge she was sitting on, and shook with fright.

"Lotta! Lotta! The bears are here, too! It's their breathing we heard. Oh, Lotta, we've found the bears! They had the sense to find this cave too, and creep into it."

Lotta was thrilled. She stumbled over to the corner and touched the bears. They were awake now, but did not mind the children at all. They knew their smell and they loved Jimmy and Lucky, who often played with them. Dobby, the half-grown bear-cub, grunted and rubbed his head against Jimmy's arm.

"Well, that's one piece of luck, at any rate," said Lotta. She sat down with her back to the furry bear. He was warm and soft. "Come on, Jimmy. Let's cuddle up to the bears. They will soon make us warm. Get on to my knee, Lucky —I'll have hot-water bottles at my back then, and a hot-water bottle on my knee too."

33

The children cuddled up to the sleepy bears. They were like warm fur rugs. The bears liked feeling the children there. They were company. They made the bears feel safe, for they had been very much frightened by the wind and the flapping white tent that had flown out of the night at them.

And there in the cliff-cave slept the five creatures all night long. Dobby and Grizel, the bears, grunted and twisted in their sleep. Lucky yelped once or twice as she dreamed of chasing rabbits. The children lay against one another, feeling the delicious warmth of the furry bodies behind them. The noise of the sea and the wind did not come into the cave. All was peace and quiet.

But how surprised Jimmy was when he awoke! Daylight crept in at the small cave-entrance, and for a moment the boy could not imagine where he was. Then he stood up and stretched himself, stiff with the night's strange bed. The bears awoke too, and Lucky leapt off Lotta's knee and licked her hands. The little girl rubbed her eyes and stared around her.

"Gracious! Where am I?" she cried. Then she remembered, and her face fell.

"Oh, Jimmy—do you think we'll get into trouble?" she said. "Let's hurry back with the bears quickly. Perhaps we haven't been missed."

"No such luck," said Jimmy, peeping out of the cave. "I say, look—there's a boat out. Perhaps it's looking for us. We'll get out of the cave with the bears and hail the boat. The tide is still swishing round the cliff."

So the two children took hold of the bears' great paws, and with Lucky behind urging them on, the great animals shuffled to the cave-entrance. They all squeezed out, and Jimmy hailed the boat below.

"Hie! Will you rescue us?"

The two men in the boat looked up and their eyes nearly fell out of their heads when they saw the children with *two bears*! They stared and they stared.

"We must be dreaming," said one to the other. But when the children shouted again, they knew they were not, and they drove their boat in closer to the cliff. They didn't mind rescuing children, but they drew the line at bears.

BACK TO THE CAMP

"WE got caught by the tide last night and couldn't get back!" yelled Jimmy to the two surprised fishermen. "We'll be down to you in a minute."

The bears climbed down the cliff-side, grunting when they slipped. Lucky leapt about nimbly, quite enjoying herself. Such adventures didn't usually happen to the little dog!

The children and Lucky were soon standing on a rock, whilst the boat rocked nearby. The men brought it nearer. They stared at the bears, afraid and puzzled.

"How did those bears get here?" shouted one man. "Are they circus-bears? Did they escape?"

"Yes; haven't you heard?" shouted Jimmy, his voice rising above the roar of the waves. "They ran away last night and we tracked them here—but the tide cut us off and we couldn't get back. So we cuddled up to the bears and spent the night in a cave. Now we want to take them back to the circus."

"I'm not having any bears in *my* boat," said one man firmly. "They might claw me."

"Of course they won't," said Jimmy, who couldn't imagine anyone being afraid of bears or of any other animal either. "Oh, do let them come—they'll only run away again if we leave them here."

"Well, you keep the bears at your end of the boat then," said the man at last. "And mind you, boy, if one of those bears comes near me, I'll push him overboard!"

"He'd be difficult to push!" laughed Lotta. "Come on, Dobby—come on, Grizel. Oh, Jimmy, it's going to be awfully difficult to get the bears in, isn't it!"

It *was* difficult, especially as the two men wouldn't help

at all. They crouched back into their end of the boat and looked really scared. Dobby playfully put out a paw to one of the men.

"No, Dobby," said Lotta, smacking the bear's paw back. "Don't try to be funny in a boat."

The bear sat himself down and the boat shook. Then Grizel clambered in, almost falling into the sea as he did so. Last of all, little dog Lucky leapt lightly in—and my goodness, the boat was as full as it could be!

Jimmy had to take the oars, for neither of the men would get into the middle of the boat to row. The bears were so heavy at their end that the other end of the boat was quite high up in the water.

"Never had a boat-load like this before!" grumbled one of the men. "Whoever heard of taking bears for a row?"

Jimmy laughed as he rowed. He was glad to be going back to the circus, though he couldn't help feeling uncomfortable inside about whether Mr. Galliano would be angry because he and Lotta had gone off without a word.

"Still, every one would guess we'd gone after the bears," said the boy to Lotta. She nodded her head. She was busy quieting the bears, who didn't much like the up-and-down movement of the boat.

"I hope they won't be sea-sick," said Lotta anxiously. But the voyage was not long enough for anyone to feel sea-sick. The boat rounded the rocky corner of the cliff, where the waves were still splashing, and came to a sandy cove. The boat ran in, and the men jumped out. They pulled the boat up the beach, and then stood at a safe distance whilst the children tried to coax the two bears out of the boat.

But, you know, they wouldn't get out! No—the movement of the boat, strange and unusual to them, had really frightened them. They were afraid to move in case something stranger happened. It was no use pulling and tugging at them. They were far too heavy to move. They squatted down in the bottom of the boat, looking like great fat fur-rugs!

"Oh, Dobby! You are a perfect nuisance!" said Jimmy,

THE BEAR SAT HIMSELF DOWN AND THE BOAT SHOOK

giving it up with a sigh. "Lotta, run up to the circus-field and fetch Mr. Volla. I don't believe anyone but him could get these tiresome creatures out of this boat."

"You stay here with them then, and I'll send Mr. Volla as soon as I can," said Lotta, not at all liking the idea of going back to the camp without Jimmy—but she saw that there was really nothing else to do.

She ran to the cliff-path and began to climb it to the top. The bears watched her. They grunted. They were glad that Jimmy and Lucky were still with them. Lucky jumped down to the bears and tried to play with Dobby, for they were very good friends. But Dobby wouldn't play, so Lucky went and had a glorious game of chase-the-waves-and-bark-at-them till one unexpectedly ran up the beach too quickly for her, and she got her legs wet. After that she stuck closely to Jimmy's heels and growled whenever a wave came near.

Lotta climbed to the top of the cliff. She saw the circus-field in the distance. It was early morning, and she did not expect people to be about. But the whole camp was up, and she could hear shouts and calls as she drew near.

She squeezed through a hole in the hedge, and looked over the field. She could hear Mr. Galliano's voice.

"Perhaps the caravan was blown off in the wind! This is a terrible time, yes! First the bears, then the children—and now Madame Prunella's caravan is gone!"

Lotta looked over the field in surprise. Madame Prunella's caravan gone? How strange! Where could it have gone to? Sure enough, the little girl could not see it. And at that very moment Sticky Stanley the clown saw Lotta! He gave a yell.

"Lotta! Here's Lotta! Where have you been, Lotta? We've been up all night looking for you and Jimmy!"

Every one crowded round the dirty and untidy little girl. Lal, her mother, came up and put her arm round her. She had been crying.

"Oh, Lotta," she said, "we've been so worried about you and Jimmy. We thought the storm might have blown you over the cliff, or something!"

"No, I'm quite safe," said Lotta. "We went after the bears, Jimmy and Lucky and I. And we found them!"

"*Found* them!" yelled Mr. Volla joyfully. "Oh, you wonderful child, Lotta—oh, you beauty!—oh, you treasure!"

Lotta laughed. Mr. Volla was hugging her for joy. He had been up all night worrying about his bears, and now he was like a child because his pets had been found.

"Where are they—where are they?" he kept asking.

"And where's Jimmy?" asked Mrs. Brown, who was looking pale and tired.

Lotta told her tale quickly. "We couldn't get the bears to move out of the boat," she finished. "So Jimmy sent me to get Mr. Volla. Can you come, Mr. Volla?"

"I come at once!" cried the bear-trainer in joy. "Oh, what a night it has been! Neither I nor my bears have slept a wink!"

"You haven't found Madame Prunella's caravan too. I suppose?" asked Sticky Stanley the clown, running alongside Lotta as she led the way to the cliff. Half the circus-folk came with them, for they all loved a bit of excitement.

"Of course not!" said Lotta. "Goodness—we would have been astonished to see Madame Prunella's caravan in that little cave along with the bears, I can tell you! How strange that she has disappeared!"

They all climbed down the steep cliff-path. As soon as they came in sight of the boat, with the bears still huddled at one end, Mr. Volla gave a shout of delight.

"Dobby! Grizzel! Are you safe? Come to Volla!"

At the sound of their beloved trainer's voice the two bears raised their heads. When they saw Mr. Volla running over the sand towards them, they scrambled heavily out of the boat and went to meet him, grunting and growling in a most comical manner.

They flung their hairy arms round their keeper, and all three danced together for joy. Jimmy began to laugh. He really couldn't help it. Then one of the bears trod heavily on Mr. Volla's foot and he yelled with pain.

That made Jimmy laugh still more—and he and Lotta went back up the cliff-path with every one else, laughing and talking, telling of their night-time adventures.

"Is Mr. Galliano angry?" he said to Oona the acrobat. "Has he sat up all night waiting for us?"

"We all have, young Jimmy," said Oona. "You can't rush off like that, you know, without being missed. You should have left word about what you were doing. Galliano is pretty down about everything this morning—the big tent is spoilt, you were missing, and Prunella and her caravan have disappeared! You know, she's a queer person—and *I* wouldn't be surprised if she's gone off in one of her tantrums because of the storm!"

By now they were all back in the camp. Mrs. Brown came and kissed Jimmy. Galliano roared to him:

"Where have you been? Why didn't you say where you were going? Boy, I've a good mind to give you a taste of my ring-whip, yes! You cannot do as you like here, no—and you take Lotta with you too. Bad, bad, very bad!"

Jimmy didn't know what to say. Every one was afraid of Mr. Galliano when he was in a temper. The boy stood there and looked pale and sulky. That didn't please Mr. Galliano at all! He put his hat quite straight on his head and glared at Jimmy.

"Your tongue is gone—yes?" he roared. "You have nothing to say to me? The bears go, you go, Lotta goes, and Madame Prunella goes! My whole circus can go for all I care!"

He cracked his whip round Jimmy's feet and the boy jumped. He had never seen Mr. Galliano quite so angry and upset before, but the ring-master had been up all night and was tired and worried.

And then Lotta, who had been standing nearby, looking scared, heard a sound that made her prick up her ears at once. It was a parrot's screech! Well, Madame Prunella couldn't be so far away then!

The little girl slipped off. She ran to where the sound seemed to come from. It was somewhere near the enormous bulk of the blown-down tent, surely! The little girl stood and listened carefully. She heard a muffled voice say, "Baked beans and tomatoes, baked beans and tomatoes," very solemnly indeed.

"That's Gringle!" thought the little girl joyfully. "But goodness me, wherever can he be?"

And then she suddenly knew where Madame Prunella and her caravan were! They were buried underneath the enormous canvas of the blown-down tent! No wonder they couldn't be seen. No wonder every one thought that Madame Prunella was gone!

The little girl rushed back to Mr. Galliano and pulled at his hand. She was very glad to stop him raging at Jimmy. Perhaps he would be in a better temper when he heard the news.

"Mr. Galliano!" she cried. "I've found Madame Prunella's caravan! Come quickly!"

Mr. Galliano forgot his temper at once. He looked down at Lotta, surprised and delighted. "Where is it—where is it?" he cried. "This is good news, yes!"

"Come and see," said Lotta, glad to see his frowns disappear. "You *will* be surprised!"

PRUNELLA IS FOUND

"COME quickly and I will show you where Madame Prunella's caravan is!" cried Lotta—and every one followed the little girl. She ran to where the great tent lay in an enormous pile.

"The caravan is under the blown-down tent," she cried. "Listen—you can hear the parrots screeching!"

Sure enough the parrots *were* screeching—and some one else was too! Madame Prunella had woken up and had tried to open her caravan door, to see why the windows were so darkened—and she found that she couldn't open the door! The heavy weight of the tent lay all around it. So Madame Prunella screeched too, and kicked hard at the door.

Mr. Galliano smiled. It was always funny when Madame Prunella lost her temper.

"All right, all right, Madame Prunella," he shouted in his enormous voice. "You shall be set free, yes. In a minute or two. So be patient!"

But that was just one thing Madame Prunella could never be! She went on kicking and hammering at the door, and she and her parrots screeched like a hundred express trains at once. Lotta and Jimmy couldn't help laughing.

Then many hands began to tug at the great tent, and presently it was moved so that Madame Prunella could open her caravan door. It flew open and a very red and angry woman looked out. She had on a bright red dressing-gown with a yellow girdle, and her shock of hair stuck up straight just like the crest of a bird.

"She's awfully like one of her parrots," grinned Jimmy. Madame Prunella heard him and she caught up the nearest thing to her hand, and threw it at Jimmy angrily. It was a saucepan—but it didn't really matter what it was, because Madame Prunella could never throw straight.

The saucepan went flying through the air, and Oona the acrobat caught it neatly. He stuck it upside down on Sticky Stanley's head, and every one laughed.

"Who shut me in? Who barred my door?" Prunella cried. Then she saw the great tent, which still lay over half of her caravan. Her eyes grew wide and surprised.

"Goodness gracious!" she said. "So that's what happened! The big tent blew down—and I never knew!"

"There are a lot of things you don't know, Prunella," said Oona, her cousin. "You must have taken your parrots to your caravan last night, and gone to sleep without knowing that the tent had frightened Dobby and Grizel, two of the bears, and made them run away. You didn't know that Jimmy and Lotta disappeared, and we spent all night looking for them! You didn't know that they've turned up again with the bears, and . . ."

"Oh, what I have missed!" wailed Madame Prunella, bursting into floods of tears. She loved any excitement, and it seemed terrible to her to think she had slept through such a lot. "How wicked of you all not to come and tell me!"

"Yes, but we didn't know where you were," said Oona. "We thought you had disappeared too! It was Lotta who found you just now—she heard one of your parrots screeching."

The parrots were still screeching, all except Gringle, who kept muttering to himself, "Bacon and eggs, bacon and eggs, bacon and eggs." Then he raised his voice to a shout and cried, "BACON AND EGGS!"

"The poor darling. He does want his breakfast," said Madame Prunella, and she ran to her caravan again to feed her parrots. They were all flying loose this morning and hovered round like a brilliant cloud of colour. Jemina the monkey was thrilled with them. She waited till one perched near her and then she made a grab for one of the bright feathers in its tail. She pulled it out and leapt away, whilst the parrot screeched and tried to claw her.

Jemina stuck the feather into the buttonhole of her little coat, chattering proudly. Every one laughed—and then

Jimmy looked at Mr. Galliano. Was he going to say any more? Had he still got a scolding or a punishment for Jimmy and Lotta? But, hurrah! the ring-master was beaming again, and his top-hat was well on one side once more. Good! He had forgotten about Jimmy, that was quite plain. Things were right again—the bears were safe, Madame Prunella was safe, the big tent was not really damaged!

"Come on, let's slip away to my caravan," whispered Jimmy to Lotta. "We're going to get off lightly this time, Lotta. Let's go and ask my mother for something to eat. I'm awfully hungry, aren't you?"

So away they went to Jimmy's caravan, and there they found Mrs. Brown cooking a big meal of bacon and sausages on her neat stove. Jimmy sniffed the smell with joy.

"Mother, weren't Lotta and I lucky not to get into real trouble with Mr. Galliano?" he began. And then he saw Mrs. Brown's face. It was very stern indeed!

"You may think you've got off very lightly with Mr. Galliano," she said sharply, "but you've got a whole lot of trouble coming from *me*, Jimmy. How dare you go off like that with Lotta, and never think of letting me or Lal know what you were doing? We have been terribly worried all night long."

"Well, we did bring back the bears, Mrs. Brown," said Lotta coaxingly, slipping a small paw into Mrs. Brown's hand. But Mrs. Brown would not take it. She was angry and hurt.

"Bears! What do I care about bears!" she cried, slapping the sausages on to a dish. "It's you two children I care about. And to think you care so little for me that you can slip off like that and leave me to worry and worry!"

"Oh, Mother—we didn't think," said Jimmy, upset to see his mother's white, stern face. "We won't do such a thing again. Really we won't. We're sorry—aren't we, Lotta?"

"Yes, *very* sorry," said Lotta, and she burst into tears, for she was tired and over-excited. Mrs. Brown set down the dish of sausages and put her arms around the little girl.

"All right," she said. "I'll forgive you both. You're just a pair of naughty, thoughtless, independent children —but you're brave and kind too, so I won't scold you any more. Now, eat up your breakfast, both of you, and I'll make you some cocoa with plenty of sugar."

The children were happy once more. They simply could not bear to see Mrs. Brown cross or worried—now things were all right again. They ate their breakfast hungrily, and Mrs. Brown fussed round them like a hen with a couple of chickens.

"And now," she said firmly, "both you and Lotta are going to curl up in those two bunks, Jimmy, and go to sleep. You look tired out, both of you. The circus is not moving for a while and there is no show to-night—so you can be lazy for once. Get off my feet, Lucky—you've had enough breakfast! Stop pulling at my shoe-laces!"

The children really were very tired, and they didn't in the least mind curling up in those cosy bunks, with Lucky and Lulu the spaniel at their feet. In half a minute they were both sound asleep, and did not even stir when Mrs. Brown knocked over a pail with a great clatter on the floor.

The circus settled down once more. Dobby and Grizel joined the other bears with great delight, and there was a grunting and smacking of paws as the two adventurous bears greeted the other three.

Madame Prunella settled down too, her fright and temper forgotten. At ten o'clock the circus-camp was just as usual, except that most of the grown-ups looked rather tired after their worrying night.

Mr. Galliano sat in his caravan with Tessa, his fat smiling wife. Every one loved gentle Mrs. Galliano, and would have done anything in the world for her. She was helping Galliano to count up the money he had taken.

Galliano sat smiling, his hat cocked over his left ear, for he wore his top-hat even in the caravan. The circus had done splendidly at Bigminton—and now the ring-master was planning how to make it even bigger and better.

"Tessa, we will have more clowns—yes?" he said happily. "Two more, three more!"

"Three more," said Mrs. Galliano. "But Sticky Stanley

must be the chief clown, Galliano. He has been with us so long and is so good."

"Yes—he shall be head clown," said Mr. Galliano. "Ah—we shall be grand with four clowns, yes! And more animals. Now what animals shall we have? Not tigers, no! They are not happy in the ring as are the bears and the dogs and horses. We will have—we will have——"

"A performing seal!" said Mrs. Galliano, who loved seals and sea-lions. "Ah, Galliano, I remember once that my uncle had a seal that loved him so much it even wanted to have a bath with him at night. But my uncle was a big man and there was not enough room for them both in the bath—so he had a great bath made especially for him, and he carried it with him wherever he went. Then his seal could bathe with him each night. How I remember seeing that great bath strapped to the top of his caravan!"

"Good! We will have a performing seal, yes," said Mr. Galliano. "And what else? Lions—no. Cats—no. Then what?"

Mrs. Galliano turned over a sheaf of papers and letters. She came to a picture of zebras trotting round in a ring. She showed it to Galliano.

"See, these are rare in a circus," she said. "Here is a picture of Zeno and his twelve trained zebras. Shall we write to him and have those? They are pretty creatures."

"Yes," said Galliano thoughtfully. "Pretty—but difficult. We shall have to keep that daring young Lotta away from them or she will be trying to ride them—and zebras will not be ridden! And see, wife—here is a photograph of the amazing conjurer, Britomart. He would be marvellous to have in our circus, yes! We will write to them all!"

"And look at these performing goats," said Mrs. Galliano, opening a booklet that showed pictures of troupes of snow-white goats. But Mr. Galliano shook his head.

"No—not goats. They smell too strong," he said. "We will have three more clowns, Britomart the great conjurer, the performing seal, and Zeno with his zebras!"

The news soon went round the camp, and the children were very excited.

"Gracious!" said Lotta, skipping round happily. "What

fun we shall have! I bet I'll ride on those zebras before they've been in the circus for a week, Jimmy!"

"And I bet I'll have that seal eating out of my hand!" cried Jimmy. "Come on—let's go and tell Madame Prunella. She hasn't heard the news yet!"

So off they ran, and soon they were talking excitedly to Madame Prunella about all the newcomers that would soon arrive. She gave them peppermints to suck, and Gringle put out a foot for one, too.

"Pickles and peppermints," he remarked solemnly. "Peppermints and pickles!" That clever old bird could always think of something quaint to say!

THE CIRCUS MOVES ON

THE circus was going to leave the field at Bigminton in a few days. The children had a nice holiday, roaming about the sea-shore with the dogs, or riding over the countryside. Lotta rode Black Beauty, her own horse, of course—and Jimmy rode a rather quiet horse belonging to Lal. He rode quite well now, but he would never ride so well as Lotta!

She had ridden horses since she was a baby. She scared many of the folk she met on their rides by suddenly standing up straight on Black Beauty's back, just as she did in the circus. People stared in alarm and surprise, and then they smiled and said:

"Oh, that must be Lotta, the circus-girl. Isn't she marvellous!"

That would please Lotta very much, and then Jimmy would tease her and say she was vain. They had great fun together, and the only thing they didn't like about their little holiday was that Mrs. Brown made them both go to bed much earlier than usual.

"You will both be in bed by half-past eight," she said firmly. "Circus-hours are bad for children. I never before in my life heard of children going to bed every night at eleven o'clock and half-past, till I came to join the circus. Now that there is no need to go to bed late for a few nights, you will both go early."

This didn't please Jimmy and Lotta at all, and the first night they both disappeared about half-past eight and didn't wander into the circus-camp again till half-past nine, very hungry indeed.

But alas for them! They were sent off to their bunks without any supper at all—though Mrs. Brown was cooking one of her most delicious stews. Jimmy saw a big tin of pineapple chunks too, a thing he loved very much. But not a bite did he and Lotta have!

"Bed at half-past eight and a good supper—bed after half-past eight and no supper at all," said Mrs. Brown. "You can choose which you like!"

So after that both children ate a good supper and snuggled down in their bunks nice and early. Lotta went to her own caravan, and Jimmy slept in his with his father and mother, Lucky, his dog, and Lulu, the old spaniel, who loved the whole family. She had once belonged to two men who were unkind to her—and so Jimmy took her for his own, and she adored him.

When the circus went on the road again, the children were happy and excited, for they knew that at the next stopping-place the new clowns and animals would be joining them. Then what a fine circus it would be!

"Oh, how I'll love playing with a seal!" said Jimmy, joyfully. "And won't it be marvellous to watch Britomart doing his wonderful tricks, Lotta."

"What *I'm* looking forward to is riding a zebra," said Lotta.

"And that is just what you won't do, no!" said a voice nearby—and Lotta looked up to see Mr. Galliano there, his hat well on one side, and his stiff moustaches sticking up well. "Zebras are not horses. They are dangerous animals. They can never be properly tamed. You will not try any tricks, Lotta, no!"

He went on his way, swinging his great whip. Lotta looked after him sulkily.

"Well, that's that!" said Jimmy. "No zebras for *you*, Lotta! I once had to promise Mr. Galliano I'd never go and play with any circus-animal till I had his permission —and you'll have to promise not to go near the zebras!"

"I didn't promise anything—and I shan't promise," said Lotta. "Zebras—what are zebras! Just little striped animals not so big as horses. I'll soon be able to do what I like with *them*!"

"Well, you jolly well be careful," said Jimmy anxiously. He knew how daring Lotta was, and although he was no longer afraid of her hurting herself, as he had once been, he didn't want her to do anything dangerous, for he was very fond of the naughty little girl.

Lotta jumped down from the caravan steps, turned herself nimbly upside down, and walked all round Jimmy on her hands, kicking at him with her feet as she passed him. She made dreadful faces and sang as she went:

"Don't go near the zebras, they'll kick you all to bits,
 Don't go near the seal in case it frightens you to fits,
 Don't go near the elephant in case you make it bray,
 Don't go near the monkeys, they'll make you run away!"

Jimmy roared with laughter. Lotta looked so funny walking round on her hands, her legs dangling over, and the song was so very silly. He rushed at the grinning little girl, but she leapt upright again and tore off to Sticky Stanley the clown. She hid behind him and he kept Jimmy off with a broom he was using. He laughed at the two excited children.

"My word, Lotta, I don't know why Mr. Galliano wants to get any more clowns!" he said. "He could take you and Jimmy for a fine pair!"

"Stanley, what other clowns are coming?" asked Jimmy, wondering if the clown had any news. Sticky Stanley sat down on an upturned bucket and told them all he knew.

"Well, the two clowns, Twinkle and Pippi, are coming," he said. "They are knock-about clowns—they knock each other over, fall off everything, and have a very funny act in which they keep a fruit-shop and end up by throwing tomatoes and everything else at one another."

"Oooh, that sounds simply gorgeous," said Lotta, delighted. "I'd really *love* to see people throwing tomatoes at one another."

"Yes—it's just the sort of thing you'd like to do yourself, isn't it," grinned Sticky Stanley, who knew what a little monkey Lotta was. "Well, the third clown is Google. He's really funny too. He has a wonderful motor-car, and everything goes wrong with it—and in the end it blows up into a hundred different pieces! Google has a fine little dog called Squib. You'll like him. He helps Google with his nonsense."

"Oh, this all sounds too lovely for words," said Lotta joyfully. "Now tell us about Britomart the conjurer."

Stanley looked rather solemn. "You mustn't tell this to anyone," he said. "But I don't like what I've heard of Britomart. Mind you, he's a remarkably clever man, and some of his tricks are so amazing that you can't help thinking he does really know a lot of magic. But I've heard he's a hard man, and unless he's given the longest time and the best turn in the ring he can be very unpleasant."

"Well, I shan't interfere with him much!" said Jimmy. "All I shall do will be to watch him at his tricks. I shan't want to meddle with his magic in case I find myself changed into a donkey or something all of a sudden!"

"Oh, that *would* be fun!" said Lotta. "I could ride you in the ring, then. And feed you with carrots!"

"Britomart once had a circus of his own," said Sticky Stanley, getting up and going on with his work. "I don't know why it came to an end, but it did. And now he travels around with all kinds of shows. It's a great thing for Galliano's Circus to get Britomart. We should draw enormous crowds. You know Mr. Galliano is getting a much bigger tent, don't you?"

"Is he really?" said Jimmy. "My goodness, what fun! We'll have hundreds and hundreds of people watching us each night now, Lotta!"

When the circus had once again settled down in camp, the children kept a watch for new arrivals. Jemina the monkey came to sit on the gate with them, and Sammy the chimpanzee joined them. He loved the children, and chattered to them in his own language, slipping his hairy paw into Jimmy's hand.

So there they all sat on the field-gate—Jimmy, Lotta, Jemina the monkey in a new green dress, and Sammy the chimp, dressed in his usual trousers and jersey. He even wore a tie, but as he much preferred it to hang down his back instead of his chest, it looked a little odd. As fast as Jimmy put the tie in its right place, Sammy put it in the wrong place. So in the end Jimmy gave it up, and Sammy proudly wore his nice blue tie down his back.

He had got a habit lately of slipping his paw into the

pockets of Jimmy's shorts, and taking out anything he found there. Jimmy missed marbles and string, pennies, sixpences, and toffee! As soon as he discovered that it was Sammy who was the thief, he made the chimpanzee turn out his own pockets—and then Jimmy took back all his things!

But Sammy was so clever at taking things without the boy knowing, that three or four times a day the chimpanzee had to turn out his pockets and give Jimmy back his belongings! This was quite a new trick and Mrs. Brown was very shocked at it.

"That's stealing, Jimmy," she said. "You must punish Sammy well if he does that."

"Oh no, Mother!" said Jimmy, just as shocked. "He doesn't know what stealing *is*. He only does it for fun. It's just a new trick with him. I couldn't punish old Sammy for that. He wouldn't understand. No—for a few days I won't put anything in my pockets at all, and he'll soon get tired of putting his hand in when he finds there's nothing there!"

So, whilst they sat on the gate, waiting and watching for new arrivals, Jimmy grinned to feel Sammy slipping a paw into his pockets. "Nothing there, Sammy old fellow!" he said. "Nothing there! Now you just give Lotta one paw and I'll take the other, and you won't be able to get into any mischief then!"

So Sammy had to sit still and quiet, a paw held by each of the children, whilst Jemina sat first on Jimmy's shoulder, then on Lotta's, and then on Sammy's, chattering monkey-language as hard as she could go!

Then suddenly Jimmy shouted loudly, "Hark! I hear trotting. It's the zebras! Zeno and his zebras, hurrah! Open the gate, Lotta, and we'll see them all trotting in!"

ZEBRAS—A SEAL—AND TWO LITTLE GIRLS!

DOWN the country road, in the hot May sun, came a fine sight—a most strange and unusual one, that thrilled the two children and made them shout for joy.

First of all came six beautiful striped zebras, led by a groom on a small horse. The zebras trotted in a bunch together, their striped coats gleaming like satin. They looked round with big eyes that had a wild gleam in them.

Then came six more zebras—and they drew a marvellous carriage, in which sat Zeno, their trainer. Zeno was a small man, dressed in riding-clothes. He had top-boots on with very high heels to make him look taller. His riding-coat was blue and his breeches were yellow, so he looked very gay. He held the reins of the zebras and held them tightly too. Zebras were not like horses, tame and biddable. They were difficult, wild creatures, who hated to be bridled and ridden, and hated to feel the drag of a carriage behind them. but every zebra loved Zeno, and was willing to do what he wanted, so they were a happy united family, and made a marvellous picture as they trotted down the country road.

They swung in at the open field-gate, and the groom jumped off his horse. He went to the noses of his zebras, and looked at his master, Zeno. Zeno got out of his carriage, which was just as brilliant as he was, for it had glittering yellow wheels, and bright blue paint everywhere else. Lotta simply longed to have a ride in it.

"Where is Mr. Galliano?" called Zeno in a commanding voice. He looked at the children, and Jimmy went over to him.

"There he is, sir—look," said the boy. "The big man

THE ZEBRAS LOOKED ROUND THEM WITH BIG EYES

with the whip. He's seen you. Can I give you any help with your zebras, sir?"

"Certainly not," said Zeno. "You don't know what you are talking about, boy. They'll bite you as soon as look at you."

He strode off in his high-heeled boots, a big top-hat on his rather small head. The groom stood patiently waiting with the zebras. Lotta went softly up to him.

"May I touch a zebra?" she asked.

"Of course not," said the man, startled. "Do you want to be bitten? Keep away, please. They are upset at the change in their surroundings and I don't want them to be handled at all. Their travelling-stables are coming along in a minute or two, and then I'll be able to give them food and drink."

The nearest zebra looked at Lotta out of its big startled eyes. Lotta looked back, and made a curious noise. The zebra pricked its ears towards her and said "Hrrrumph!" rather like an old man sneezing. It reached out its head to Lotta, and the groom jerked it back.

"Get back, Zebby," he said. "It's no good you pretending you want to make friends with the little girl. You only want to bite her fingers off."

"Oh, but he doesn't," said Lotta. "He really doesn't. Please let me stroke his satiny nose. He's so lovely."

Mr. Galliano caught sight of the children standing near the zebras, as he strode over with Zeno to look at them. He shouted at Lotta.

"Now, you bad little girl, didn't you promise not to touch those zebras, yes! Go away at once before I come after you. Jimmy, you can help Zeno sometime with his zebras, for all animals are good with you, but not to-day whilst they are upset at strange surroundings. Go with Lotta."

"Oh, if that isn't too bad!" cried Lotta indignantly, as she and Jimmy moved away. "To think you can help with the zebras, and I can't. I can manage horses much, much better than you, and you know it."

"Yes, but zebras aren't horses," said Jimmy with a grin.

"Ha ha! You won't be able to touch the zebras now you've had to promise not to."

"Jimmy, I tell you I *haven't* promised," cried Lotta. "I know Mr. Galliano said just now that I had—but I haven't, so there! He's made a mistake."

"Well, you'd better tell him so then," said Jimmy.

"I shan't," said Lotta. They stood and watched Zeno showing his fine collection of zebras to Mr. Galliano. At first they shied away from the big ring-master—but, like most horse-like creatures, they liked him, and he was able to rub one or two sleek noses before he nodded to Zeno and strode away.

Then, a few minutes later, the big travelling-stables arrived—great vans, whose sides could be opened or shut. They came into the field, and the groom and Zeno were soon very busy getting the tired animals into their stalls. They had trotted a long way that day to join Galliano's Circus.

"Well, that's the first new arrival," said Jimmy. "Now we'll watch for the seal, Lotta. Come on. Who's bringing it, I wonder?"

The performing seal was due to arrive that afternoon too—but it was rather disappointing when it did turn up. It came in a closed van, and as it passed into the field the children heard the swish of water inside.

"It travels in a tank of water," said Lotta. "I never thought of that. Oh, Jimmy, we'll peep and see what it's like as soon as the van is opened. I say, look—who are those two little girls?"

Behind the van came a caravan, driven by Pierre, the owner of the seal. He was dressed in ordinary clothes, and was whistling a merry tune. He was a cheery man, with a red face and the brightest blue eyes the children had ever seen. Riding on the very top of the caravan were two little girls.

"Oh! I didn't know there would be any children," said Lotta, pleased. "It'll be fun to play with them, won't it?"

Jimmy wasn't so sure. He was quite content with Lotta, and he didn't want any more little girls in the circus. So he didn't say anything, but just looked at the two girls. One was about the same age as he was, and the other looked older. They grinned down at the two circus children from the top of the caravan.

"That's rather a good place to ride," said Lotta. "I never thought of that before."

"It does look rather good," said Jimmy. "But I can't see my mother letting me ride on the top of *our* caravan."

Pierre, the owner of the performing seal, had a thin little wife with curly red hair, as well as his two little girls. They sprang lightly down from the top of the caravan, and Mrs. Pierre looked from the window.

"Jeanne! Lisa!" she called. "Are you all right?"

The girls took no notice of their mother at all. They were bold little things, pretty, with red curls like their mother. They were very dirty and untidy, and their smiles were very broad indeed.

"Hallo!" said Lisa, tossing her red curls. "Do you belong to this circus?"

"Yes," said Jimmy and Lotta together.

"It doesn't look much of a camp," said Jeanne, looking round. "We've been used to much bigger circuses than this. I call this rather a poor show."

"Go back to a better show then," said Jimmy, unexpectedly rude. He felt that he disliked these little girls with their red curls, bold faces, and loud voices.

"Oh, *isn't* he polite," said Lisa, and she giggled. Her mother called her again, and she took no notice at all.

"Your mother's calling you," said Lotta.

"She can call then," said Jeanne rudely. At that moment her father came up, and heard what she said. He gave her a slap and she squealed.

"Go and help your mother," said Pierre, with a scowl on his red face. The two little girls went off, sulking. Pierre looked at Jimmy and Lotta and Lucky.

"You must be the two Wonder-Children," he said. "Pleased to meet you."

"Can we see your seal?" asked Jimmy eagerly. Pierre's wife and the girls had gone to the van and were letting down one side. Inside was an enormous tank full of water that gleamed a deep blue. In the tank swam a beautiful seal. Jimmy ran to it. The seal popped its head out of the water and looked at Jimmy with the most beautiful eyes he had ever seen. He loved the seal from that very moment.

"Oh, isn't it lovely!" cried Jimmy. "I do love its eyes. What's its name?"

"Neptune," said Pierre, pleased that Jimmy liked his seal. "He's the cleverest and best seal in the world. Aren't you, Neptune?"

The seal made a strange noise and nodded its head. The children laughed. The seal seemed to laugh too, and then, diving into its tank, swam gracefully round and round, up and down, to and fro, its tail acting as a rudder to guide it.

"Would you like to feed him?" asked Pierre. "Neptune! Dinner!"

With a gobbling noise Neptune shot up to the top of the tank. Pierre took down a bag from a nail and gave it to Jimmy.

"Throw him a fish," he said. Jimmy opened the bag and found many fishes there. He picked one out and threw it to the watching seal. Neptune caught the fish deftly and then looked for another.

One after another he caught the fish, never missing once. "What a marvellous cricketer he would make," said Jimmy.

"Does he come out of his tank?" asked Lotta.

"Oh yes!" said Pierre. "He comes into the ring with me. He and I play cricket—and he never misses a ball, as you can guess. He *is* a marvellous cricketer. He is a wonderful balancer too. He can balance a pole on the tip of his nose —and a ball on the tip of the pole!"

"Oh no!" said Jimmy, not believing this at all.

"Well, wait and see," said Pierre, and he twinkled his bright blue eyes at them. "Now I must see Mr. Galliano and find out where I can put my caravan."

He went off to Mr. Galliano's caravan, and left Jimmy and Lotta watching the seal. It popped its head out again and made a soft noise to Jimmy. He went into the van, reached up to the top of the tank and stroked the seal's wet nose. In a trice it was right out of the tank, flapping itself round Jimmy's legs. The boy got a real surprise.

"Get back!" he cried in alarm, but the seal took no

notice. It pushed itself against Jimmy's legs and nearly knocked him over. Then Jeanne and Lisa came up, and they rapped on the top of the tank with a stick.

"Hup, hup!" they cried in circus language, and the seal "hupped," and got back into the water.

"You'll get into trouble if you make my father's seal get out of the tank," said Lisa.

"I didn't make it. It got out itself," said Jimmy crossly.

"Crosspatch!" said Jeanne, and she pinched Jimmy. The little boy shook himself free and walked off in a huff with Lotta.

"I wish those girls hadn't come," he said. "I'm not going to like them one bit. Promise you won't make friends with them, Lotta."

But that was another promise Lotta wouldn't make. She laughed at Jimmy and ran off to help Laddo with the horses. Lotta was certainly a little monkey these days.

THE THREE NEW CLOWNS

THE circus was not going to open for two weeks, because Mr. Galliano wanted all the new performers to settle down, make friends with one another, and practise their turns in the ring together.

The three new clowns were to arrive the next day, and Britomart, the conjurer, was coming the day after. Lotta and Jimmy felt too excited for words.

"Do go and chatter somewhere else," said Mrs. Brown, shooing them off the steps of her caravan. "You are much worse than those screeching parrots."

The parrots were excited, too, by the arrival of more animals and performers, and they screeched and chattered all day long. Madame Prunella had had to move her caravan a little farther away, for not all the circus-folk would put up with such a dreadful noise!

"Swee-ee-eep!" cried one parrot mournfully. "Swee-ee-eep!"

"Sounds as if he thinks Madame Prunella's chimneys want sweeping," grinned Jimmy. "Just listen to old Gringle, too!"

"Sausage and smash, sausage and smash," said Gringle loudly.

"You've got it wrong, old boy. It's sausage and *mash*," said Jimmy, running his fingers down the parrot's soft, feathery neck. But Gringle preferred sausage and smash, and said so, at the top of his voice.

The zebras soon settled down in the camp. Jumbo the elephant was delighted to see them. He trumpeted loudly to them whenever they passed and they whinnied back. Most of the animals liked good-tempered old Jumbo, and Sammy the chimpanzee was so fond of him that he scrambled up on Jumbo's back whenever Mr. Tonks, his keeper, was not there to stop him.

The performing seal was quite ridiculous with Jimmy. It went completely mad whenever the boy appeared, and made little snickering noises of joy. It always leapt out of the tank at once, and Jimmy had to stop it from following him all over the field.

The two girls, Jeanne and Lisa, were jealous because their seal loved Jimmy. It took no notice of either of them at all, just as they took no notice of their mother. Jimmy wondered what his mother would say if he wouldn't come when he was called, or ran off without doing his jobs, or was as rude to her as Jeanne and Lisa were to their mother.

Jimmy was rather hurt because Lotta went about so much with the two girls. She giggled with them and went to look at the two beautiful dolls that some one had once given them. Jimmy felt quite left out, and he went off with Lucky to watch for the arrival of the three new clowns. He sat on the fence alone, with Lucky licking his boots every now and then. He thought it was a great pity that Jeanne and Lisa had come.

Soon a fine caravan appeared. It was painted red, and on its wooden walls were posters showing the two clowns, Twinkle and Pippi. They looked very funny with their enormous eyebrows, big red noses, wide mouths, and large ears. They grinned out of the pictures at Jimmy, and he was so busy looking at them that he nearly fell off the fence when a tousled head stuck itself out of a caravan window and yelled at him:

"Boy! Are we near the circus-camp?"

It was Twinkle, one of the clowns. But he was not dressed up now, nor was his face painted like a clown's. He was just a jolly-faced man with big bulging eyes and a shock of yellow hair.

"Yes. You're there!" said Jimmy, jumping down. "Are you Twinkle or Pippi?"

Another head stuck itself out of the window—and to Jimmy's great surprise it was exactly the same as the first one! It had a shock of yellow hair and big bulging blue eyes with a merry twinkle in them.

"Hey," said the first head to the second head. "This boy wants to know if I'm Twinkle or Pippi. Which am I?"

"Well, if you're Twinkle, I'm Pippi, and if I'm Pippi, you're Twinkle," said the second man solemnly. They looked at one another in such a comical manner, their eyebrows working up and down together, that Jimmy burst into roars of laughter, and Lotta came running up to see what the joke was.

Twinkle and Pippi came out of their caravan and grinned at the two children. They were exactly alike, even to the dimples in their right cheeks.

There was a roar of welcome from the circus-field, and Mr. Galliano came striding up. Twinkle and Pippi were old friends of his. He shook hands with them, slapped them on the back, and took them to his own caravan to see Mrs. Galliano.

"I like Twinkle and Pippi," said Jimmy. "We'll have some fun with them, Lotta."

"Pooh! They are not such good clowns as *we* have often seen in other shows," said Lisa's mocking voice. Jimmy turned away. He hated the way that Lisa always mocked at everything. She had even laughed at little dog Lucky, and said that once she had seen a dog who was far cleverer than Lucky.

"And you'll see what will happen when she is three years old," she said. "Her brain will go! She won't be able to do so well as she does now. You wait and see!"

"Don't say such horrid, untrue things," said Jimmy, picking Lucky up in his arms.

All four children waited to see if Google, the third clown, would come along. Sure enough he did. He drove a van, with a caravan towed behind it.

"What's in the van, I wonder?" said Lotta.

"That motor-car of his that falls to bits!" guessed Jimmy. "What fun! Do you suppose it's Google driving the van? He's got a dear little dog with him."

It *was* Google. But Google out of the circus-ring was quite a different person from Google *in* the ring. He was a sharp-faced, bad-tempered little man, and the only creature he really loved in the world was his dog Squib.

He hated children, and gave all four a scowl as he drove his van carefully in at the gate.

"I don't much like the look of *him*," said Jimmy. "He looks as if he'd like to eat us all."

"But his dog is a dear," said Lotta. "Squib! Squib!"

The dog in the driving-seat pricked up his ears when he heard his name called, but he did not leave his master's side. Lucky yelped to him, but he did not yelp back. He was not going to make friends with anyone until he had had a good sniff round the camp, and made sure whom he would like to know! He was a very particular little dog, and so fond of his master that he even went into the ring with him and did his best to help, though he was always frightened by the *bang* that came when the motor-car burst into bits!

Britomart was not coming until the next day, so it was no use waiting to see any more people arrive. The children wandered round the camp, saying cheeky things to the parrots, looking admiringly at the zebras, and getting Neptune most excited by telling him that fish, fish, fish was coming for his dinner. He flapped out of his tank and flippered himself eagerly around Jimmy—and he would *not* go back into his water.

So the little boy walked off—but the seal followed him, working itself along on its flippers quite fast.

"Oh, do go back, Neptune," said Jimmy in alarm. "I shall get into trouble if you follow me about like this."

The seal looked at Jimmy out of beautiful brown eyes and made little loving noises. It seemed to think that Jimmy was the most marvellous person it had ever met, and for the first time Jimmy wished that an animal didn't like him so much!

He tried to dodge it by running round a caravan, diving under a cart, coming up the other side and jumping up the steps of his own caravan. But the seal followed him faithfully, and heaved himself up the steps of the caravan. Jimmy had shut the door—and the seal hit it hard with its nose.

"Come in!" cried Jimmy's mother, who was peeling potatoes. She had no idea there was a seal out there. Neptune hit the door such a bang with his nose that it flew open with a crash—and with many delighted noises the seal flippered itself indoors.

"Bless us all, what's this coming in!" cried Mrs. Brown, in a fright. "It's the seal! Good gracious, whatever next? Does it think it's invited to dinner, or what? Really, what with parrots and monkeys and chimpanzees playing around, I've no time for seals! Jimmy, tell it to go out. It's shaking the caravan to bits, galloping round the floor like that."

Jimmy couldn't help laughing. The seal was doing its best to get on to his knee, it seemed. Jimmy got up and went out of the caravan. "Come on, Neptune," he said to the seal. "You can't go rushing about like this. You really must stay in your tank."

He met Pierre as he took the seal back to its tank. Pierre was cross.

"What do you mean by taking Neptune off like that?" he demanded. "He'll come to harm, and he's very valuable."

"I didn't take him," said Jimmy. "He just jumped out and followed me."

"Lisa said you took him," said Pierre, still very cross. The seal had gone to his side and was trying to take its master's hand in its mouth. It was a very loving, friendly creature, and nobody could help liking it.

"Well, Lisa told a story then," said Jimmy indignantly. "She's a naughty girl. I *didn't* take the seal. You had better make Lisa sit by the tank and guard the seal all day long. She hasn't enough to do."

Pierre went off with Neptune, and Jimmy saw Lisa peeping round a van at him, delighted because he was angry. He ran at her and she disappeared at once.

He went to see Twinkle and Pippi. They had already made friends with Sticky Stanley and were talking eagerly about what they could all do in the ring, for they were to work together. Google was to have a turn to himself. Stanley was pleased about this, for he had not much liked the sulky look of the sharp-faced third clown.

Jimmy stayed and listened. Twinkle and Pippi were so alike to look at that he still didn't know which was which

—and if he asked them, they pretended not to know either, and asked one another who they were, and scratched their heads and worked their eyebrows up and down till Jimmy went into fits of laughter.

"They are twins," said Stanley. "No one has ever found out yet which twin is which—and I certainly don't know, and never shall know. They even have exactly the same freckles!"

Only Britomart the great conjurer was to come now—and then, the day after that, the circus was to open again, this time with all its new performers. My goodness, what a show it would be! Jimmy and Lotta could hardly wait for the night!

C

BRITOMART JOINS THE CIRCUS

THE conjurer did not arrive till the evening of the day before the circus was due to open again. He drove up in a most magnificent car. It was blue, with silver edgings, and the whole of the inside was blue and silver too.

Britomart was dressed in ordinary clothes, but he looked a most magnificent man, even in a dark blue suit and grey hat. He was very tall, taller than Mr. Galliano, and he had even more marvellous moustaches. His eyebrows were jet-black, and so bushy that they jutted out over his eyes. His eyes were strange. They were as black as his hair, but they glinted coldly, like steel, whenever he looked at anyone. He never seemed to smile, and all four children felt rather afraid of him.

He got out of his magnificent car and went to talk to Mr. Galliano. He was very haughty with the ring-master, and did not even shake hands with him. As for kind Mrs. Galliano, he did not even say good-evening to her.

Soon a marvellous van arrived, carrying the conjurer's circus belongings. It was blue and silver, like the car, and across it was painted one word, in enormous silver letters:

BRITOMART

"Golly! Isn't he grand! " said Jimmy. "Nobody as grand as this ever came to Galliano's circus before. He must be very rich."

"He is," said Lisa, who always knew everything about everybody—or pretended to, if she didn't. "I'm surprised he came to a tuppenny-ha'penny circus like this! I can't imagine why he did! "

"For the same reason as *you* did, I suppose," said Jimmy

crossly. "To make some money! To hear you talk, anyone would think you owned all the circuses in the world. Hold your tongue for a little while, Miss Know-All!"

Lisa put out her tongue at Jimmy, and put out her arm to pinch him slyly. But he was ready for her and skipped out of the way.

Britomart was not going to sleep in the camp. He was going to stay at the biggest hotel in the town, and would only come out to the circus each evening, when the show began.

"Good thing too," said Sticky Stanley. "That man may be made of magic—but he gives me the creeps with those glinting black eyes of his!"

Every one was very busy the next day. The enormous new tent was already up, and Brownie and the other men had seen that it was safe as could be. They did not want it to be blown off the ground, like the other one. Many new benches had been bought, and were arranged round the ring.

Even the ring itself was new, for Mr. Galliano had ordered new plush sections, which, when fitted together, made a bigger ring than before.

The programme was carefully worked out. It would be longer than usual, because there were more performers, but the tickets were to cost more. Each performer was given his time and his turn, and a rehearsal was planned and carried out in the morning.

Every one did well. Only Britomart was not there. He would never come to rehearsals, and as he was so famous, he was allowed to do as he liked. Jimmy and Lotta were in a great state of excitement. Lucky was thrilled to think that the show was beginning again, for she, like all the other animals, loved the excitement of the ring.

The first night came. The big towns near the camp knew all about the show, for Mr. Galliano had sent his men to paste up enormous circus-posters all over the place. So every one knew, and hundreds of people came to see the first show. They streamed in at the big gates, where they got their tickets, and made their way to the big tent. Flaring lights lit up the inside, and big shadows danced in the roof.

The band tuned up. The drummer rolled his sticks on the drum softly. Jumbo trumpeted somewhere, and some of the parrots screeched joyfully. They loved to go into the ring with Madame Prunella, they loved the clapping and shouting and cheering, just as the circus-folk loved it.

The show began. The circus-parade went round the ring —horses, performers, dogs, carriages, everything, bowing and waving—and then the first turn began.

It was Lal and Laddo, with their beautiful horses—and how they waltzed, how they cantered, how they stood up altogether on their hind legs, their heads magnificent with great clusters of ostrich feathers. Jimmy thought they had never done so well before.

One by one all the turns came on. Sammy and Mr. Wally —Lilliput and his monkeys—Prunella and her parrots— Lotta and Black Beauty—and then Pierre and his performing seal.

That seal! It was simply marvellous! It galloped in beside Pierre, who was now perfectly wonderful in silver and gold. Neptune was cleverer than a dog! He did everything he was told. He sat on a stool. He galloped round the plush ring on his flippers. He played cricket with his master, catching the ball every time that Pierre sent it into the air.

He balanced a long pole on the very tip of his nose, and then Pierre placed a ball on top of the pole. And do you know, Neptune went round the ring with the pole on his nose, and the ball balanced safely on the tip of the pole! Jimmy couldn't imagine how he did it.

He had another trick too. Pierre brought in six bells hung on a brass rod—and what do you think Neptune did? He struck those bells with his nose, and played "Jack and Jill went up the hill" on them! How the people cheered!

"Marvellous!" said Jimmy, as the seal galloped out of the ring beside Pierre, trying to catch hold of his fingers as he went. "How I do like that seal! I'd love one of my own."

The zebras were beautiful to watch too. They trotted in, and played a kind of football match, deftly kicking the ball from one to the other.

"They look just like football players with striped jerseys

on!" said Jimmy to Lotta. "Oh, look—Zeno is going to do something else."

So he was. The trainer got three of the zebras together, and leapt up to their backs. He put one foot on each of the outside zebras, so that he was straddled over the third one. Then, at words of command, all the other zebras took their places in front of him, and his helper threw him up the reins. And round the ring with his twelve zebras galloped Zeno, standing safely on the backs of two of them, with a third in the middle, below!

Every one knew how difficult zebras were to tame and train, and the watching people shouted and cheered Zeno till they were hoarse. The parrots outside the ring got most excited when they heard all the noise, and they joined in the cheering too.

"Hip-pip-prah!" shouted the parrots, till Madame Prunella scolded them and made them stop. Even then Gringle kept shouting loudly, and Prunella had to take him away for a while, till he became quiet.

The clowns were an enormous success. Jimmy laughed till he cried when they built up a fine greengrocer's shop, and piled it full of fruit and vegetables, falling over one another all the time, bumping into things—and then, at the end, getting terribly angry with one another, and throwing all the fruit and vegetables about.

"Squish, squish," went the tomatoes. "Thud, thud," went the turnips. "Smack, smack," went the oranges. Really it took quite three minutes to sweep up the ring after that ridiculous performance. Twinkle and Pippi enjoyed it just as much as the audience, and they came out grinning and laughing, their hair plastered with tomatoes!

"Wouldn't you like to join us in our turn, Jimmy?" grinned one of them. Jimmy didn't know if it was Twinkle or Pippi, for they dressed exactly alike for the ring. Stanley pretended to throw a tomato at Jimmy, and the little boy ducked, afraid of spoiling his grand circus-suit.

He and Lucky were a great success too. Lucky could walk the tight-rope as cleverly as any clown, and she could spell words with letters, which always made people shout with amazement.

TWINKLE AND PIPPI ENJOYED IT JUST AS MUCH AS THE AUDIENCE

The thing that always astonished people more than anything else was when Jimmy asked his little dog one question —"Which is the finest circus in the world?"

And from the mass of big black letters Lucky always picked out the one word—"Galliano's!" That made people stand up and cheer, and Jimmy and Lucky bowed happily round the ring before they ran lightly out.

Britomart the conjurer was perhaps the most astonishing performer of all. He strode into the ring looking like a giant, for he wore big heels to his boots and a great feather in his hat, and as he was already tall, he looked enormous.

He had a strange deep voice, too, that seemed to come from his boots. He was not only a marvellous conjurer but a juggler too. He could take twelve golden balls and throw them one by one into the air, and never let them drop, keeping them circling up and down like a golden fountain. He could throw sharp knives in the air too—three, four, five at a time—and catch them neatly by the handles, one by one, as they came down. It was astonishing to watch him.

His conjuring was wonderful as well. Jimmy and Lotta, who were watching him closely from the curtain that hung at the ring-entrance, could not imagine how he did his tricks.

Britomart had a small table on which was a golden cage. The cage was empty. There was nothing in it at all. The conjurer sent his helper round the ring to show the empty cage to the people.

Then, at a deep word of command, the air was full of canaries! They fluttered out of nothing, it seemed, and flew all around the conjurer's head! At another word of command they entered the golden cage one by one—and then, strangest of all, at a third word, they completely disappeared from the cage, and it was empty once again!

"However did he do that?" cried Jimmy. "Where have the birds gone?"

But that was not the only strange thing that the magnificent Britomart did. He took a pair of top-boots and placed them in the middle of the ring, after having sent his helper

71

round to show the watching people that the boots were empty and quite ordinary.

But dear me, were they quite ordinary? No, they were not! For as soon as Britomart placed them in the centre of the ring, and shouted a word of command, those boots began to dance! How they danced! It was simply amazing to watch them.

"They're alive!" said Lotta, half afraid. "I never saw a thing like that before. Goodness, isn't he clever!"

Britomart certainly was. After he had juggled and conjured for twenty minutes, he bowed and strode off, followed by the loudest cheers Jimmy and Lotta had ever heard.

"And all the time he never once smiled," said the little girl. "What a strange and clever man he is! All the same, I hope we don't have too much to do with him, Jimmy."

But they were going to have a lot to do with Britomart, though they didn't know it!

POOR MRS. GALLIANO!

THE circus, with its new performers, was an enormous success. The third new clown, Google, was perhaps the silliest of all the turns, but he made people laugh till they cried. He was a very solemn person in the ring, and somehow this made people laugh all the more.

He had a most extraordinary car, which he drove into the ring, with his little dog Squib sitting beside him. After the car had gone once round the ring it began to make the funniest noises. Bells rang inside it, something fizzled, and a terrible clanking noise began. This all made Google look more solemn than ever. His enormous eyebrows shot up to the top of his forehead with surprise.

Squib jumped out and went under the car. Google got out too, and as he got out, the car began to give shivers and shakes, which shot Google out on to his nose. He pretended to be very angry about that. Then streams of black smoke came from the car, and Google and Squib ran to get a pail of water. Of course Google fell over and Squib got the water all over him. He barked with rage and tried to bite Google's wide clown-trousers.

Then the car ran all round the ring by itself, with Google and Squib panting after it, calling to it, and whistling as if it were a dog. Jimmy and Lotta laughed till the tears ran down their cheeks and on to their collars! They had never seen a car running away and being whistled to like a dog before.

Well, Google caught it at last, and tied it firmly to a post, so that it shouldn't run away again. He lay down flat and got underneath it. The car then ran backwards and forwards over Google, and he shouted and yelled for all he was worth. Squib pulled him out, and they both sat down

73

solemnly to think what they could do next with this extraordinary car.

Then Google pulled all the insides out of the car and threw them down in the ring. When he had finished he got back behind the steering-wheel, and hooted the horn to make Squib get out of the way. He started up the engine —and the whole car flew into bits with an enormous BANG! The wheels came off and rolled all over the ring! The back of the car fell off. The front of the car hopped away. The seats fell out. It was the funniest sight that the people had ever seen in their lives!

And there was poor old Google sitting on the ground still holding the steering-wheel, with all his car fallen to bits around him, looking sadder and more solemn than ever. No wonder the audience yelled and shouted and clapped. No wonder Squib wagged his tail happily at so much applause. Jimmy made his own hands ache with clapping, and he wished that Google would do his turn all over again.

But he didn't, of course. He and the other clowns collected the car-pieces and went out, Google bowing and smiling all the time, pleased at his success.

"We're lucky, Lotta," said Jimmy joyfully. "We shall see Google doing that every night, as often as we like—the children in the audience are lucky if they see it once."

The children who had paid to see the circus looked at Jimmy and Lotta in surprise and envy when *they* went into the ring each night. How marvellous to be dressed like that, and have such a wonderful dog as Lucky, and such a lovely pony as Black Beauty!

"You must be very happy," a boy said once to Jimmy. "What a fine life you have!"

"It's not as easy as it looks," said Jimmy. "Circus-folk have to work hard and practise every single day! I work just as hard as you do, and harder!"

The circus-show was so good that the big tent was crowded each night. The weather was fine, and many coaches and buses were run to the circus-field from the distant towns. Mr. Galliano was delighted. Although he had to pay the new performers a great deal of money, it didn't matter, because so many more people came to see the circus that there was always plenty of money for every one to spend.

The new performers settled down well together, and got on splendidly—all except Google the clown and the two little girls Lisa and Jeanne. Google was certainly bad-tempered, and never made a joke outside the ring. As for Jeanne and Lisa, they were two spoilt, bad-mannered children whom nobody liked. They were always playing tricks on Jimmy, and trying to get him into trouble.

Lotta liked playing with them, and this made Jimmy cross and unhappy. Lotta had always been his very own friend, and he hated sharing her with anyone.

"Why do you go and play with those silly dolls belonging to Lisa and Jeanne?" he grumbled. "Why don't you come with me and fly my new kite? Dolls are babyish."

"No, they're not," said Lotta. "I like dolls. I've never played with them before—only with dogs and horses. You can come and play with the dolls too, if you like, Jimmy."

"Pooh!" said Jimmy rudely. "*I'm* not a baby, if *you* are!"

This wasn't a clever thing to say to Lotta, who could be very obstinate when she liked, so off she went and played all the more with Lisa and Jeanne. Mrs. Brown was sorry to see this, because she knew that the two red-haired girls were bad for Lotta. They were teaching her to be rude and cheeky, and to be disobedient too. Lal, Lotta's mother, could never manage the wilful little girl very well, but Mrs. Brown could—yet now she found that Lotta was being rude to her, and disobeying her whenever she could.

Britomart the conjurer had very little to do with the circus-folk. He came and went without a smile, never said good-day to anyone, and only spoke to Pierre, whom he had worked with in another circus. Every one was rather afraid of him, and even the animals did not seem to like him, which was unusual in a circus.

Jumbo twitched his big ears restlessly when Britomart passed by. Sammy chattered angrily at him. Jemima ran away. Lucky growled.

"There's something queer about Britomart," said Jimmy

to Lotta. "Lucky likes nearly every one, but she doesn't like the conjurer! Black Beauty doesn't like him either. He shied at Britomart when you rode near him yesterday, Lotta."

Zeno and his zebras were soon very much liked. He and Mr. Tonks and Mr. Volla made friends, and put their caravans close together. Twinkle, Pippi, and Sticky Stanley were soon very friendly, too, and they all liked Madame Prunella very much, and often sat outside her caravan with her, eating one of the wonderful curries she made. She had been in many hot countries to get her parrots, and had learnt to make all kinds of queer dishes, which the three clowns loved.

Google did not make many friends, but Squib was soon a great playmate for Lucky. Those two dogs really loved one another, and played "He" and Hide-and-seek as often as they could. Lucky even began to take part of her own dinner to share with Squib, who did not have quite such good meals as Jimmy gave to Lucky.

One morning Jimmy met Mr. Galliano as he went across the field to see to the dogs with Lotta. To his great surprise Mr. Galliano had his top-hat on quite straight. This always meant that the ring-master was upset about something, and Jimmy wondered what it was. Jimmy was going to ask him a question, when Mr. Galliano pushed the boy roughly aside.

This astonished Jimmy so much that he stood and stared. Galliano was never rough like that. The ring-master saw him staring and shouted at him.

"Have you no work to do, boy? Then you will do it at once, yes, and not stand gaping like a hungry dog!"

Jimmy scurried off, and Lotta went with him, rather frightened. "Whatever's the matter?" she said. "What *can* be upsetting Mr. Galliano? Didn't he look angry?"

The children soon knew what the matter was. Mrs. Galliano was very ill. Sticky Stanley the clown told them, and he had heard it from Madame Prunella, who had been called to Mrs. Galliano in the night.

"Mr. Galliano thinks the world of his wife," said Stanley, sewing a black bobble on to his clown's suit. "The doctor is coming soon, and until he has been and gone, you had better keep out of Galliano's way."

So Lotta and Jimmy kept well out of the way—but Jeanne and Lisa didn't, and got well slapped for running into him round a caravan. They ran howling to their mother.

"Serves them right," said Jimmy, pleased. "They could do with a lot of slappings, those two. I wish I could give them a few!"

Mrs. Brown went to see if she could help Mrs. Galliano, who lay in the big bed in her caravan, looking white and ill. Nobody knew what was the matter with her, and every one was very worried, for they all loved the fat and gentle Tessa.

"Do you suppose she will have to go away from the circus?" Jimmy asked. His mother, Mrs. Brown, nodded her head.

"I'm rather afraid so," she said. "She does seem very ill, and she would not be able to stand the noise and excitement of the camp, or go on the road when it moves."

The doctor came at last. He stayed a very long time with Mrs. Galliano, Madame Prunella, and the ring-master. When he came out of the caravan putting on his gloves, he looked rather grave. Mr. Galliano followed him, the tears running down his cheeks and soaking his moustache. The two watching children were alarmed. They had never imagined that Mr. Galliano could shed tears.

They did not like to see him so sad, and they ran to Jimmy's caravan. Mrs. Brown went to hear the news and she soon came back and told them.

"Poor Mrs. Galliano is very ill indeed," she said. "She has to go to hospital and see a very famous doctor, who may be able to help her. She keeps saying that she won't leave Galliano, so goodness knows what will happen!"

"But she can't stay in that caravan if she is so ill," said Lotta. "Whatever will happen?"

The whole circus was worried and upset. They did not dare to talk to Galliano, who strode up and down, biting at his moustache, his hat perfectly straight. Then he went into the caravan and shut the door.

When he came out again, he called Mr. Wally, Mr. Tonks, and Lilliput. They went over to him, serious and quiet.

"Boys," said the ring-master, "I am not going to leave Mrs. Galliano. I am going with her. She cannot stay here, she must go to a hospital, yes—but I cannot let her go alone."

"We're awfully sorry about it, sir," said Mr. Tonks, looking as unhappy as poor Mr. Galliano. "But what about the circus? It must have a ring-master!"

"Yes," said Mr. Galliano. "I have not forgotten that. You will have a ring-master—it will be Britomart!"

BRITOMART, THE MAN WITHOUT A SMILE

So Britomart the conjurer was to be at the head of the circus! Mr. Tonks, Mr. Wally, and Stanley looked at Galliano in dismay. None of them liked Britomart, though they knew he was very clever indeed, and had had a circus of his own.

"Britomart knows how to run a circus," said Mr. Galliano. "He will do it well, yes! The show is running splendidly now, and it will go on for weeks. Perhaps by the time you are all on the road again I shall come back with Tessa—yes?"

Nobody said anything. They all felt upset at losing both Mr. and Mrs. Galliano, but they could not beg him to stop behind and let Mrs. Galliano leave alone. The three men looked at the ground, and Mr. Tonks blew his nose so loudly that it almost sounded like Jumbo trumpeting.

Then Mr. Wally spoke. "When are you going, sir?" he asked. "To-day?"

"This morning," said Mr. Galliano. "Tessa must go at once, the doctor says. A car is coming for her presently —I see it coming in at the gate now, yes! Now, my friends, you will all do your best for Britomart—you will promise me this—yes?"

"We'll do our best," promised Mr. Wally, Mr. Tonks, and Stanley. They shook hands with their ring-master, and with serious, solemn faces watched Madame Prunella, Mrs. Brown, Lal, and a nurse put Mrs. Galliano comfortably in the big car. She smiled bravely at every one. Then Mr. Galliano, still wearing his riding-breeches, coat, and top-hat, but without his whip, got into the car beside the driver.

All the circus-folk came running, for now the news had spread like wildfire around the camp.

"Galliano's going! Galliano's going! Quick, come and say good-bye!"

They all poured out of the caravans, and rushed to wave good-bye—the grooms, Brownie, Pierre, Jeanne, Lisa, the clowns, Mr. Volla, Jimmy, Lotta, Lucky, and Lulu the spaniel—what a crowd there was running beside the big car as it slowly and carefully drove out of the field, with Mr. Galliano waving and trying to smile.

Then down the country road it went, still slowly, so as not to jolt Mrs. Galliano. It disappeared round the corner, and every one looked sad.

Lotta began to cry. She was very fond of Mrs. Galliano. Jimmy put his arm round her. "Cheer up, Lotta," he said. "Mrs. Galliano will soon be better—and then Mr. Galliano will be back, and everything will be fine again."

There was a loud honking down the road and a great blue-and-silver car swept up to the field-gates. It turned in, and jolted slowly over the field.

"It's Britomart!" said Lotta, drying her eyes. "*Isn't* he tall!"

The conjurer seemed even taller that morning. His jet-black eyes gleamed under his bushy eyebrows, as he looked all round the field.

"Where is Mr. Wally?" he called. Mr. Wally came up.

"I want a meeting of all the chief performers," said Britomart. "Then I shall go round the circus and see everything. I shall take the Gallianos' caravan for mine, and live in the camp, now that I am to be ring-master."

"Certainly, sir," said Mr. Wally. Sammy came up behind his keeper, and slipped a hairy paw into his.

"Take that chimpanzee and put him into his cage," ordered Britomart. "In my circuses performing animals are not allowed to wander about the field loose."

"But, sir, Sammy often does," said Mr. Wally, in surprise. "He's like a child. He plays with the children and is as good as gold. He mopes if he is shut up always."

"I am master here now," said Britomart in a cold sort of voice. "Shut up the chimpanzee, please."

Mr. Wally went off with Sammy, his face as black as thunder. Mr. Galliano had never ordered him about—and here was Britomart giving him orders before he had been in the camp two minutes.

"Tell two or three women to clean out Mr. Galliano's caravan for me, and to stack their furniture into an empty van," said Britomart to Brownie, who was nearby. "I have some of my own things coming this afternoon."

Brownie went off to tell Mrs. Brown to get some one to help her clean out the caravan. Mrs. Brown hurried to find Lal, and the two women began to take out the furniture for the men to store away.

Jimmy and Lotta hated seeing everything being taken out of the caravan they knew so well. The big bed was taken to pieces, and the blankets rolled up. Even the pictures were taken down from the wall. They were only coloured posters of the many circus-people that the Galliano's knew, but they made the walls gay and bright and interesting.

Britomart went to look at the horses. He loved horses, and they stood perfectly still whilst he stroked each fine animal and spoke to it. But no horse nuzzled to him as they did to Lotta and Jimmy, Lal and Laddo.

Lotta came running up to Black Beauty whilst Britomart was there with the horses. She jumped up on to his back and rode him away. Britomart called after her in his deep voice:

"Lotta! Where are you going?"

"For a ride over the hills," said Lotta.

"No circus-horse is to be taken for pleasure-riding," Britomart said. "Bring him back."

"But he is my own horse!" cried Lotta. "My very own. I can ride him whenever I like."

"He may be your own but he belongs to the circus," said Britomart. "And whilst I am ring-master you will obey my rules and my orders, little girl. Bring that pony here."

Lotta tossed her black curls, her face red with anger. She was about to gallop away when Jimmy, who had been listening, caught hold of the bridle.

"Don't be silly, Lotta," he said in a low voice. "You'll

81

only get yourself into trouble. Take Black Beauty back. You know quite well that any ring-master has the right to make his own rules."

Lotta struck Jimmy's hand away from the bridle, but he put it back again, and firmly led the horse to where the others stood. Lotta was so angry that she would not say a word to either Britomart or Jimmy. She slipped out of the saddle and ran to her caravan, her face still bright red. How dare anyone say she mustn't ride Black Beauty over the hills! Why, she did it every day.

"That is a spoilt girl," said Britomart. "She must do as she is told, or I will not let her go into the ring."

"Good gracious!" thought Jimmy in dismay. "Not let Lotta go into the ring—he must be mad! Whatever would Lotta say? I'd better warn her to be careful."

He went off to find Lotta. Britomart called a meeting of all the performers, and soon they were around him, listening to what he had to say. Only Lotta and Jimmy were not there.

Jimmy had found Lotta on the bed in her caravan, thumping at the pillow in anger, pretending that it was Britomart. The boy couldn't help smiling.

"Lotta! Don't be so silly! You'll have feathers flying all over the place."

"I wish it was Britomart's hair I was thumping off!" said Lotta fiercely. "I hate him! Horrid cold man without a smile."

"Lotta, just listen to me for a moment," said Jimmy, sitting on the bed.

"I won't," said Lotta, and she thumped Jimmy. He pushed her away.

"You *must* listen," he said. "Do you know what Britomart said just now? He said if you didn't do what you were told he wouldn't let you go into the ring."

Lotta stared at Jimmy in horror. "Not let me go into the ring!" she cried. "Not let me ride Black Beauty in the circus every night! How dare he say that!"

"Lotta, do be sensible," said Jimmy. "You know that any ring-master gives his own orders and they must be obeyed. Lal and Laddo will tell you that."

Lotta was still in a rage. She turned sulky and wouldn't say another word. She wouldn't promise to be good, she wouldn't even say she would try. In the end Jimmy left her, feeling rather cross himself. He joined the circus-folk around Britomart, who had been altering the programme of the show.

There was no doubt that Britomart was a very clever man. Most of the alterations he made were excellent. Mr. Galliano was a fine ring-master, but rather free and easy, willing to let the circus-folk do as they liked providing that their work was good and they were happy. Britomart only cared about whether the work was as good as it could possibly be—the happiness of the people came second or not at all.

Twinkle and Pippi found that their act was cut down. Google's was made longer. Jumbo's was cut shorter, and the performing seal was given longer. Though some of the people grumbled, most of them thought that Britomart certainly knew what he was doing.

That afternoon a van drew up with Britomart's belongings in it. Jimmy and Lotta, Jeanne and Lisa, stared in amazement. They had never seen such grand furniture for a caravan before. There was even a clock made of silver, with little black elephants running all round it. The children stared wide-eyed as the things were taken into the caravan.

"Get away," commanded Britomart, when the children crowded too near. "Get right away. You are not to come near this caravan. It is private. If I catch any of you near it, you will be sorry."

Britomart looked so fierce that every child scurried away at once.

"I guess no one will be asked to call in and see Britomart in the evenings," said Jimmy.

But he was wrong. Pierre was the only one that Britomart liked, and he invited him to his caravan many a time. Sometimes Neptune the seal went with Pierre, and it was funny to see the great creature flipping itself along beside its master.

No one else ever chatted to the new ring-master. He

lived alone in the caravan, and not even Jemima the monkey dared to play a trick on him.

Lotta called him "The man without a smile," and it was a name that suited him very well. He made a magnificent ring-master when the show opened each night, tall and commanding, and he could crack his whip even more loudly than Mr. Galliano.

But nobody liked him—and how they all missed jolly Mr. Galliano and his gentle wife, Tessa!

"If only they would come back," Lotta sighed a dozen times a day. "If only they would come back!"

LOTTA GETS INTO TROUBLE

THE circus stayed for a long time in the same camp, for it drew hundreds of people each night, and there was no need to move. Everything in the show went well. Britomart was really an excellent ring-master, and everything ran like clockwork.

But outside the circus things were not quite so good. For one thing, Britomart never praised anyone, and the circus-folk could not get along happily without a good word. Galliano had always praised them and their animals generously, and his people loved that and worked all the harder for him. But Britomart only spoke when things went wrong, and then he found fault sharply.

Lotta was the first one to get into trouble, and it was because of the zebras. The little girl would *not* keep away from them, and they seemed to like her and welcomed her with joy whenever she slipped into their travelling-stables. Soon she was able to stroke every one of them, and Zebby even learnt to push his black nose into her hand.

Lotta never went into the stables when Zeno or his man were about, for she knew that she would be ordered out. She went secretly, not even telling Jimmy.

One day she jumped lightly on to the back of one of the zebras. It reared up in surprise, and snapped round—but when it knew it was Lotta, it stood quietly, though trembling a little.

"I believe I could ride you, Zebby," whispered Lotta in delight. "I believe I could! Just wait till Zeno takes you into the ring to-morrow, and I'll try!"

So, the next day, when Zeno took his zebras into the ring for their daily practice, Lotta was there. Zeno tied a bunch of zebras together outside the ring, and took six of them inside. Lotta ran to the bunch and loosed Zebby.

In a moment she was on his back! He reared up, and then galloped into the ring! Lotta clung on his back, delighted.

Zeno looked up and saw her, and his eyes nearly dropped out of his head. No one had ever ridden Zebby before! Zebby was nervous and difficult, and sometimes was not even taken into the ring in case he should upset the others.

Zebby flew round the ring with Lotta on his back—and at that very moment who should stalk in to speak to Zeno but Britomart himself!

Lotta didn't see him. She was busy wondering if she dared to stand up on the zebra's back as she stood on Black Beauty—but even as she wondered this the zebra saw Britomart standing silently at the side of the ring, and was frightened.

It stopped suddenly—and Lotta was thrown right off his back. She landed on her feet, like a cat, with a jerk. Then Britomart began to roar. He had a very deep voice that sounded as if it came from his boots, and it rang like thunder in the ring.

"Zeno! Were you not told that no one but you and your helper were to handle your zebras? How dare you let Lotta ride one! It is a most dangerous thing for a child to do."

"I'm sorry, Mr. Britomart," said Zeno, who had been as amazed and surprised as Britomart to see one of his zebras ridden by Lotta. "I'd no idea she was even in the tent. But, Mr. Britomart, it's wonderful. No child has ever ridden a zebra before. I tell you I couldn't believe my eyes!"

"Can I ride a zebra in the ring, when Zeno does his turn?" cried Lotta, delighted at Zeno's praise. "I can manage any of them, really I can—but Zebby——"

"Hold your tongue!" thundered Britomart, frowning at Lotta. "You will certainly not ride a zebra. You are a bad child to have tried. You might have frightened the animal and upset all of them. Go to your caravan for the rest of the day."

"Oh, but——" began Lotta indignantly. She had no chance to say another word, for Britomart took hold of her shoulder, shook her well, and marched her to the tent-opening. She gave a cry of rage and rushed off.

She found Jimmy and told him all about it, angry and hurt. "I only rode a zebra!" she cried. "And even Zeno said it was a wonderful thing for a child to do."

"But you promised Mr. Galliano that you wouldn't ride the zebras," began Jimmy. Lotta shook back her hair and interrupted him.

"I didn't promise, I didn't promise," she cried. "You're not to say I did when I didn't. If I'd promised I would have kept my word. But I didn't, I didn't, I didn't!"

"All right, all right," said Jimmy. "Well, Lotta, the best thing you can do is to keep to your caravan for the rest of the day, as Britomart said. If you disobey you will certainly be punished."

"I'm NOT going to keep in the caravan all day!" cried the furious little girl. "I'm going to get Black Beauty and ride him over the hills. That's what I'm going to do. And Britomart can do what he likes. He may rule everyone else in this circus, but he won't rule *me*!"

And the wild little girl ran off to get her horse, not caring at all what anyone said. Jimmy knew that when Lotta was in one of these moods it was no good trying to stop her. He watched anxiously to see whether Britomart would see her taking Black Beauty, but the conjurer was still talking to Zeno in the big tent.

Lotta galloped off alone on Black Beauty. Jimmy wandered about, kicking a stone round the field, little dog Lucky at his heels. The circus didn't seem the same any more. People were not so jolly, and Britomart seemed everywhere, with his black eyes, black moustaches, and deep voice.

Suddenly Jimmy wondered if Britomart would go to see if Lotta was in her caravan. It would not be like him to give an order, and then not see if it was carried out. He would be sure to try and find out where she was.

Jimmy ran to Lotta's caravan. She lived in it with Lal and Laddo. He opened the door. There was no one there.

It was an untidy, rather smelly caravan, not a bit like the spotless, tidy one his mother had. Jimmy looked round. He saw Lotta's bunk against the far end, and went over to it.

He grinned a little to himself. He took a pillow from Lal's bunk and put it in the middle of Lotta's. Then he took a saucepan and put it at the top of the pillow for a head. Then he pulled the blanket up—and the pillow and saucepan underneath looked just like some small person lying in the bunk.

"Good!" thought Jimmy. "If old Britomart takes a look in, he'll think that's Lotta in the bunk!"

He slipped out and shut the door. He waited till he saw Britomart come out of the tent. The conjurer looked for Lotta's caravan, and walked over to it. As he came up to it, Jimmy rapped on the door and cried, "Lotta! Come out and play!"

Then he listened as if he heard someone answering him. "Oh, do come out!" he cried, just as Britomart came up.

"Lotta has to stay in her caravan all day," said the ringmaster sternly. "It is no use asking her to come out."

He opened the door and looked in. He saw what he thought was Lotta lying in the bunk at the far end, and he shut the door. He strode off, his whip under his arm. He was quite sure that Lotta had obeyed him and was in her caravan! He did not guess that the little girl was at that very minute galloping over the hills miles away!

"If only Lotta doesn't come galloping into the field in front of Britomart!" thought Jimmy.

Luckily for Lotta she didn't. She came back just as Britomart had gone off to the town in his big blue-and-silver car. Jimmy rushed to meet her, and hurriedly told her all that had happened.

"Britomart *really* thinks you were in your bunk all day!" he said.

Lotta was hungry and tired, and not quite so bold as she had been when she rode off. She slipped off Black Beauty and began to rub him down.

"Thank you, Jimmy," she said. "Oh dear, I do so wish Galliano would come back! I know I'm going to get into trouble with Britomart nearly every day. I just feel it in my bones!"

"Come and have some cocoa and biscuits," said Jimmy. "There are some waiting for you."

It was Madame Prunella who next got into trouble with Britomart. He said that she must keep her parrots quieter. They screeched all day long.

"As for that bird who yells 'Butter and eggs' or 'Pickles and peppermint,' he's a perfect nuisance," said Britomart. "You must move your caravan right to the other end of the field."

"It is too far for me to get water from the stream," said Madame Prunella obstinately, and she would not move at all.

When Britomart saw that she had not moved even an inch, he went angrily over to her caravan. Prunella saw him coming, and smiled a secret smile. She knew how to deal with angry men who shouted.

"Talk, parrots, talk," she said in a low voice, as Britomart came nearer. And at once, altogether, the parrots talked! They not only talked, they screeched, yelled, squealed, sang, and recited.

"Plum pudding and custard!" squealed Gringle, right in Britomart's ear. "Plum pudding and custard!"

"Twice one are two, twice two are three, twice three are four!" shouted another parrot.

"Wipe your feet and put up your umbrella!" screeched a big red-and-grey bird.

Britomart shouted to Madame Prunella, but the screeching more than drowned his voice. Not a word could be heard.

Prunella put her hand behind her ear politely, as if she were trying to do her best to hear what Britomart said. The conjurer shouted again, in his very deepest voice. But no sooner was one word out of his mouth than the whole of the parrots started off again. All the circus-folk stuck their heads out of windows and doors to see whatever was the matter.

When they saw what was happening they grinned and chuckled. They knew quite well that Prunella was playing one of her favourite tricks on an unwelcome visitor. Britomart would have to go away without telling Prunella anything!

He stamped his foot and turned away angrily. The parrots screamed after him, and Gringle did a laugh exactly like Twinkle the clown's.

"Well, Prunella won *that* game!" said Oona the acrobat, with a laugh. "It's not often anyone can win a victory over Britomart!"

LOTTA MAKES NEW FRIENDS

WHEN Lal and Laddo heard that Lotta had disobeyed Britomart, and had taken Black Beauty out on the hills, they were angry with her.

"You know well enough that however hard an order is, you have to obey the ring-master," said Laddo sternly to the little girl.

"But Black Beauty is mine. I've always ridden him whenever I liked," said the little girl sulkily.

"And as for riding the zebras, it is absolutely forbidden," said Lal. "You must be mad to try such a thing."

"Zebby didn't mind. He liked me on his back," said Lotta.

Poor Lotta! She was angry and hurt because every one scolded her. She had always been made a fuss of, she was one of the Wonder-Children—and now things were quite different. The little girl ran to tell Jeanne and Lisa all about it, and they, of course, were not at all good for her.

"You do as you like!" said naughty Lisa. "Britomart wouldn't dare not to let you go into the ring! He knows how all the people love to watch you."

"You're jolly lucky," said Jeanne. "We'd simply love to go into the ring—and we can both ride very well, you know—but we haven't any horses of our own."

Lotta had sometimes let the two girls ride on Black Beauty, and it was quite true that they rode well. They could not do all Lotta's wonderful tricks, but they were clever enough in their own way, and pretty, with their red curls and upturned noses.

Lotta went about more than ever with Jeanne and Lisa. They encouraged her to disobey, to be sulky and rude. Mrs. Brown became very angry with her.

"You are getting quite impossible, Lotta," she said, when the little girl answered her rudely. "I can't imagine what has happened to you. You used to be such a nice helpful child, and now you have altered so much I can hardly believe it is the same little girl."

Lotta did not dare to be rude to Britomart, but she tried hard never to go near him, and she always ran away if he came near her. She spent a lot of her time with hot-tempered Madame Prunella, who was always pleased to tell Lotta how she had tricked Britomart by making her parrots screech so loudly that he could not make his voice heard.

"Listen, Lotta," said Prunella to the little girl, who was sitting on the caravan steps, whilst Prunella sat in a wicker-chair outside, eating an orange. "I want you to hear something I've taught Sally, that green-and-red parrot over there. Sally! Say your piece!"

The parrot cocked his head on one side, and said:

> "There was a young lady of Riga,
> Who went for a ride on a tiger."

"No, no," said Madame Prunella impatiently. "Your *new* piece, Sally—your new piece. Come on now—Britomart . . ."

> "Britomart
> Thinks he's smart,
> But he's got a stony heart!
> Britomart
> Thinks he's——"

chanted the parrot, and then stopped suddenly as Prunella shook her finger at him. Britomart was coming across the field! Daring as Madame Prunella was, she was not brave enough to let Sally go on singing that song at the top of her loud parrot voice! Sally stopped singing and looked at Lotta.

"Pip-pip-pip-pip-pip!" she said solemnly.

"She's heard that on the wireless," said Madame Prunella. "Stop it, Sally."

"Irish stew and Scotch eggs," said Gringle loudly.

"Oh, he's off again," said Prunella. "You'd be surprised at the amount of food he knows, Lotta. Every one has taught him something!"

Britomart had gone to see Mr. Wally. Since he had told him that Sammy was not to run loose, the chimpanzee had been kept in his big cage. He was puzzled and unhappy about this. He sat huddled up in a corner and looked very miserable. Jimmy went to play with him every day, and Lucky popped in to say how-do-you-do, but the chimpanzee missed wandering round the circus, in charge of either Mr. Wally, Jimmy, or Lotta.

Lilliput, too, had been told that Jemima the monkey must be kept on a lead, or else she too must keep with the other monkeys, who had a big cage of their own in Lilliput's caravan. Jemima had been used to leaping about all over the camp, playing tricks on every one, even on the other animals—but Britomart said she upset the zebras by sitting on their backs, and so Lilliput now had to keep her on a lead. She sat on his shoulder as he went about, and flew into tempers at times because the lead would not let her go bounding off as she pleased.

"Now, Jemima—now, Jemima," said Lilliput to the impatient monkey one morning, as she tugged at the lead and tried to bite through it. She wanted to go and talk to the parrots, whom she loved—but Lilliput had other things to do, so she must stay with him.

Britomart came by, and Jemima chattered rudely at him. The conjurer sat down on a bench and began to tell Lilliput of a good idea he had thought of for a new trick. Lilliput listened. Britomart's ideas were usually good.

"I have a little silver-and-purple carriage, which I once used for a trick," said Britomart. "I think that it would look amusing, Lilliput, if we put two of the dogs to draw the carriage, and let your four monkeys ride in it round the ring, when all the performers parade at the beginning of the show. Jemima could drive the carriage—she is so clever that you could easily teach her this."

Lilliput thought it was a fine idea. He knew Jemima would simply love to drive her own little carriage!

"Thank you, sir," he said. "That's a good idea. I'd like to have the carriage, and I'll teach Jemima in a few days. I'll talk to Lal and Laddo, and choose two of their sharpest dogs."

Jemima suddenly jumped from Lilliput's shoulder to Britomart's, just the length of her lead. She snatched off Britomart's hat, and jumped back to Lilliput's shoulder. She put it on to her master's head—and it went right over it, right over his nose, and right down to his chin! He couldn't see anything at all.

Britomart did not even smile. Jimmy, who was nearby, laughed till he cried at the sight of Lilliput buried under Britomart's big hat—but the conjurer merely put out his hand, took his hat again, slapped Jemima, and stalked off, putting his big top-hat on carefully.

Lilliput told Jimmy Britomart's idea, and both of them agreed that it was a good one.

"Could Lucky be one of the dogs?" asked Jimmy. "And I know the best one to choose for the other—old Punch! He'd do anything for me. I once saved his life, you know, and he's always been willing to learn any new trick that I wanted to teach him. Lotta! Lotta! Come here a minute! I've something to tell you."

"I'm going to play with Lisa," said Lotta.

"Oh, do come just a minute," begged Jimmy. "It's something interesting, Lotta."

Lotta left Lisa and came over. She listened whilst Jimmy told her of Britomart's new idea.

"I think it's silly!" she said. "I think all Britomart's ideas are silly. I won't help you with Punch at all."

"Oh, Lotta!" said Jimmy, in dismay. "You really might! It would be so much easier if you would help me. We could teach the dogs quickly then."

"Well, I just shan't," said Lotta. "I won't do anything for horrid old Britomart."

She ran off to join Lisa, and told her what Jimmy had said. "You're quite right to say you won't help," said Lisa, who didn't like Jimmy. "Let Jimmy do it by himself."

All the same Lotta felt rather sorry she had been so determined not to help, when she saw Jimmy and Lilliput teaching Lucky and Punch to draw the beautiful little silver-and-purple carriage. Once the dogs knew what they were to do, they simply *flew* round the ring, with the carriage jerking behind them.

JEMIMA PUT BRITOMART'S HAT ON HER MASTER'S HEAD

"Hie, hie! Not so fast!" yelled Jimmy. "You are not race-horses! Come back here, and trot slowly."

Then the monkeys were trained to sit in the carriage—and Jemima sat up on the little driving-seat, as proud as could be, holding the reins in her tiny paws. She even clicked to the two dogs, just as she heard Lilliput click to them. Off went the tiny carriage, rumbling round the sawdust ring, the dogs trotting beautifully, Jemima driving and clicking, the other three monkeys sitting quietly on the seat together.

Jimmy laughed to see them. Britomart came in to watch. He was very pleased, but he did not say so, nor did he smile or laugh.

"I don't believe he *can* smile!" whispered Jimmy to Lilliput. "I don't think he knows how to. Wouldn't we all get a shock if he grinned at us!"

Jemima was not on a lead just then, for she had been driving round the ring. When she saw Britomart she made a little chattering noise, bounded from her seat, jumped up on to his shoulder, and once again snatched off his hat! It was all done so suddenly that Britomart hadn't time to stop her. He roared angrily at her.

Jemima darted up a steel ladder set up for Oona the acrobat, and perched the big top-hat right at the top. Then she darted down again, giggling in her monkey-way, and went to Lilliput's shoulder.

"Climb up and get my hat, boy," commanded Britomart. So, with many chuckles that he really couldn't stop, Jimmy climbed up and took down the big top-hat, keeping a sharp eye on Jemima in case she made a dart at it again.

Every one was waiting anxiously for news of Mrs. Galliano. At last the postman brought a letter for Mr. Tonks and he opened it eagerly. If *only* it would say that Mrs. Galliano was better, and that Mr. Galliano was coming back!

Mr. Tonks read the letter out loud to the circus-folk, who came gathering round to hear it.

"DEAR TONKY," said the letter,—"This is to say that Mrs. Galliano is a little better, but it will be a long time before she is well. When she leaves the hospital she must go away to get really well, so I shall go with her and have a holiday for the first time in my life. I hope the circus is doing well, and that every one is doing what they can to help Britomart. I miss you all very much, yes, and I long to be back.

"My good wishes to you all.

GALLIANO."

So Galliano was not coming back for a long time! Every one was sad and disappointed. They said nothing but went slowly back to their work.

"It's not Galliano's circus any more, it's Britomart's!" said Jimmy to Lotta.

"It isn't, it isn't, it isn't!" said Lotta fiercely. "I won't have it called Britomart's!" And she stamped her foot so hard that her shoe button flew off and nearly hit Jimmy on the nose!

LISA PLAYS A TRICK

THE circus went on doing very well, although the circus-folk did not like their new ringmaster. Only Pierre, and Google the clown, seemed to like him, and they talked to him, and even laughed, though Britomart did not smile with them any more than he did with the others.

Pierre's performing seal was a marvellous creature, and Jimmy and Lotta really loved it. It was so gentle and loving, and so clever that it seemed to know what trick to do before it was even taught.

Pierre had taught it to blow a tune on a whistle, and the seal loved to play the tune over and over again. It was the tune of "Yankee-doodle went to town," and very soon all the parrots were whistling it too. Everybody got very tired of "Yankee-doodle" and begged Pierre to teach the seal something else.

But it was Jimmy who taught Neptune to play "God Save the King," and the seal was cheered and clapped in the ring, when he came flipping in after the last turn, and set the band going with whistling "God Save the King" on his own whistle!

Lisa and Jeanne were jealous of Jimmy because the seal liked him much better than he liked them. This was not surprising, for the two girls were not so patient as Jimmy, though they were quite kind to Neptune. The seal still tried to follow Jimmy everywhere, and he had to shut the door behind him whenever he left the big tank, or else Neptune would be out of the water and galloping after him gaily!

Once Britomart had seen the seal going after Jimmy, and had ordered him to take Neptune back at once.

"How many times in this circus do I have to say that

performing animals are not to be allowed loose in the camp!" he thundered. "Pierre! Report this boy to me if he lets your seal loose again. I tell you I will be obeyed in my circus!"

Pierre took Neptune back. "I know he *will* try to follow you," he said to Jimmy, "but you mustn't let him. You must remember to lock the door after you, when you leave him."

"I did *shut* the door this morning," said Jimmy.

"That's not enough," said Pierre. "Neptune can get the handle in his mouth and turn it. He is as clever as twenty dogs!"

"All right, Pierre," said Jimmy. "I'll always remember to lock the door."

So he did, because he had a good memory, and rarely forgot anything that he was told. Every day, when he went to see Neptune, he carefully locked the door behind him after he had said good-bye.

Jeanne and Lisa were always teasing Jimmy. They jumped out at him round corners. They poured jugs of water over him as he passed by the window of their caravan. They told him that Lucky wasn't the cleverest dog in the world, and Lisa told him all about other dogs she had known, all of which could do far more marvellous things than Lucky.

"I believe you are making all these stories up!" said Jimmy impatiently. "Everything you know of is always better, more marvellous and wonderful than anything *we* know. I'm tired of listening to you!"

He went off. Lisa made a face after him. "Bad-tempered boy," she called. "I suppose you think you're Britomart, stalking off with a scowl like that!"

"Let's pay him out for not believing all we say," said Jeanne. "Lotta! Come here! We're thinking of a trick to play on Jimmy."

Lotta was an angry little girl these days, not friends with anyone except Madame Prunella and Jeanne and Lisa. She nodded to Jeanne. "All right," she said. "What trick shall we play on Jimmy?"

"I know!" said Lisa. "Next time he comes to call on

Neptune, and locks the door behind him, we'll unlock it again—and Neptune will go galloping after him, and maybe Britomart will see him and scold Jimmy hard."

Lotta shook her head. "No, that's not a joke," she said. "I don't think I want to do that."

"Don't be so silly," said Lisa impatiently. "Of course it's a joke! We'll do it to-morrow."

Lotta said no more, but she made up her mind she wouldn't share that trick. It was a mean trick. She didn't mind a joke, but she wasn't going to play a mean trick on Jimmy.

Next morning Jeanne, Lisa, and Lotta were sitting on top of Pierre's caravan. They had an old rug up there, and all three little girls loved to lie on it, basking in the sun, playing with the dolls. Lisa saw Jimmy coming along, with Lucky at his heels as usual.

"Here he comes," said Lisa in a low voice. "We'll play the trick on him that we planned yesterday."

"I don't want to," said Lotta at once. Lisa laughed at her.

"You're afraid to," she said. "Hallo, Jimmy! Come and play up here."

"No, thanks," said Jimmy. "You and Jeanne pushed me off last time. If I came up, I'd push *you* off, and then you'd howl the place down. I hate girls that howl."

He went in to talk to Neptune, who was most excited at hearing Jimmy's voice. He came to the top of the tank, and rested his head there, looking at the little boy out of loving brown eyes. Jimmy talked to him.

"You've the whitest whiskers I ever saw! You've the brownest eyes in the world! You're the cleverest seal that ever lived!"

Neptune loved hearing all this. He put his big head on Jimmy's shoulder and heaved such a sigh that he nearly blew the boy's ear off!

Then Brownie, Jimmy's father, called him from the other end of the field. "Jimmy! Come and help me to get some water, will you?"

There was a stream at the end of the field, and the circus-folk got their water from it. All the horses and animals had to have their drinking-troughs cleaned out and refilled each day. It was quite a job to do them all, and Jimmy and Brownie were usually very busy until they had taken water to every caravan and cage.

"Coming, Dad!" shouted Jimmy. He gave Neptune one last pat and went out of the van. He carefully turned the key in the lock and went across the field.

No sooner was he gone than Lisa slipped down the side of her caravan, ran to the van and unlocked the door. The seal was out of the tank, butting the door with its nose, as it always did when some one left it. When it heard the key turn again, it took the handle in its mouth and twisted it to one side. The door opened!

By this time Lisa was on top of the caravan again, giggling with Jeanne. Lotta watched the seal gallop out of the doorway, and go after Jimmy. She did hope that Britomart wouldn't come along at just that moment!

Just as Jimmy was dipping a big bucket into the stream, something plopped into the water with a big splash. He turned in surprise—and there was Neptune, swimming joyfully in the water!

"I say, Dad, look! Neptune is having a fine old swim!" cried Jimmy. "I wonder if Pierre let him out. I locked him in just now."

The seal loved the stream. It rolled itself over and over, made funny grunting noises, and tried to catch a small fish that darted by.

Just then a shout went up from Neptune's caravan. Pierre had come along, and had found the door open and the tank empty.

"Where's Neptune?" he yelled. Lisa answered him from the top of the caravan:

"Over in the stream, playing with Jimmy."

Pierre was so annoyed that he fired off a lot of queer-sounding words in French that Lotta couldn't understand at all. Britomart put his head out of his caravan not very far off, his black eyes almost hidden by his frowning eye-brows.

"Pierre! What is the matter?" he called in his deep voice.

"Matter enough!" shouted Pierre. "That boy has taken my seal to swim in the stream!"

Britomart came out from his caravan, and walked over to Pierre. "First it is Lotta who disobeys, and now it is Jimmy," he said. "We will see what he has to say, the disobedient rogue!"

Jimmy was astonished to see two such angry men beside him, one pouring out grumbles, the other sternly demanding why he had taken the seal.

"I didn't take him," said Jimmy. "I went to see him as usual, and I locked the door after me. I really did. Someone must have unlocked it, Pierre. The next thing I knew was seeing the seal splashing about in the stream, and I thought Pierre must have let him out."

"I think you are not telling the truth," said Britomart in his cold voice. "In future you will not go into the cages of any animals excepting the dogs and the horses. Is that quite clear?"

"Oh! but, sir, can't I go and play with old Sammy, and the bears, and Jemima?" said Jimmy. "I really must. They do so love it, especially Sammy, now he's shut up."

"You understand my orders, I think!" said Britomart. "If you disobey I shall know how to punish you. Pierre, take the seal back."

The three girls had watched all this from the top of the distant caravan. They did not know what was being said, but they guessed that Jimmy was getting into trouble. When Britomart came up with Pierre and the seal, Lotta slipped down the opposite side of the caravan and ran away.

Pierre waited till Britomart had gone into his own caravan and then he looked up at the two watching girls. He knew how they disliked Jimmy.

"Did you girls unlock the door after Jimmy had gone?" he asked. He did not see Jimmy nearby, carrying a pail of water. Jimmy heard the question and looked up.

"Lotta slipped down and unlocked the door, to play a trick on Jimmy," said Lisa. This was not the truth, but the naughty little girl wanted to make trouble between Lotta and Jimmy.

Jimmy heard what she said and went very red in the face. What! Lotta played that mean trick on him! Oh no, it couldn't be! He couldn't believe it. Lotta would surely never, never get him into trouble. He went on his way, very puzzled and upset.

"I don't believe it," thought Jimmy stoutly. "Lotta wouldn't do that. And yet—she's changed so much lately. She's even horrid to Mother, and she used to love her. Perhaps she *did* do it—and wanted me to be punished for it. What will old Sammy do if I don't go and see him? Oh, it's too bad. Lotta's horrid and mean!"

And so, although Jimmy could hardly believe that Lotta would play such a mean trick on him, and didn't *want* to believe it either, he ended by thinking that what Lisa said was true.

"Everything's gone wrong since dear old Mr. Galliano went," thought the boy sadly. "*You* won't change, will you, little dog Lucky? Promise me you won't!"

And Lucky said "Wuff!" in her loudest voice, which meant, "I'll always be the same!"

PRUNELLA LOSES HER TEMPER

LOTTA did not know that Lisa had told such an untruth about her. She was soon very puzzled because Jimmy did not seem to want to speak to her, or even to look at her; as for joking with her as he used to do, or slipping his arm through hers, those were things he never did now.

"I suppose he is still cross because I play with Lisa and Jeanne," thought Lotta, frowning. "Well, why shouldn't I? I've never had girls to play with before, and I do like their dolls. I wish Lisa and Jeanne would give me one—I've never had a doll of my very own."

Jimmy was not at all happy. It was dreadful to think that Lotta had got him into trouble on purpose. He didn't go near her if he could help it, though when they practised together for their turn in the ring with Lucky and Black Beauty, they had to be with one another. But they did not need to practise this turn very much, for they knew it so well. So they got through it as quickly as possible, and then Lotta went as usual to play with Lisa and Jeanne, and Jimmy went to help his father.

He was not unhappy only because of Lotta. He was unhappy because he had been forbidden to go into any of the animals' cages. He couldn't play with the bears. He mustn't visit Sammy the chimpanzee. He couldn't go near Neptune. He didn't even like to peep in at Lilliput's monkeys, who were now in their cage all day.

The only thing he could do was to go and talk to Mr. Tonks, whose big elephant, Jumbo, was tied by the leg to a great tree. Jumbo was too big to go in a cage. He was out in the field, and was always pleased to see Jimmy. He lifted the boy on top of his huge neck, and gently blew his hair up straight—a favourite trick of old Jumbo's.

"Cheer up, Jimmy," said Mr. Tonks, seeing the boy's dull face. "You look as gloomy as a wet hen."

"Well, Mr. Tonks, things aren't the same since Mr. Galliano went," said Jimmy. "You know they aren't."

"My boy, I've seen lots of changes in my lifetime," said little Mr. Tonks. "It doesn't do to worry about them too much. You can get used to anything."

"But I don't want to get used to some things," said Jimmy. "Look at poor old Sammy, moping in his cage all day long—not even *I* am allowed to go and play with him now. It isn't good for him after being allowed free. And you know how the bears loved me to go and play with them. The cub, Dobby, cries after me when I go by without playing with him."

"Yes, that isn't good," said Mr. Tonks, lighting his pipe. "Britomart can put on a fine circus-show, but he doesn't understand animals as you and I do, Jimmy—or as Mr. Galliano did. You know, you don't usually find as much freedom in a circus as Mr. Galliano allowed in this one— so you miss it and feel unhappy about it. Cheer up—you'll soon get used to it."

"Well, anyway, I can come and have a talk to old Jumbo," said Jimmy, scratching the elephant's thick skin with a laugh. "Britomart said I wasn't to go to any animals in a cage, except the dogs and horses—so as old Jumbo isn't in a cage I can still come and play with *him*!"

"Hrrrrumph!" said Jumbo, exactly as if he understood what Jimmy was saying.

"Do you like Britomart, Mr. Tonks?" asked Jimmy after a bit.

Mr. Tonks looked round to make sure nobody could hear him.

"No, I don't," he said. "Few people do—and Britomart doesn't want to be liked. He only wants to be feared. There are a few people he is nicer to than others, because they can be useful to him—Pierre, for instance, and Google the clown, who have both done him good turns in other circuses."

"How strange not to want to be liked," said Jimmy. "I

don't want to be afraid of Britomart, but I believe I am, Mr. Tonks."

"You don't need to be afraid of anyone, Jimmy—a clever, honest, good-natured boy like you!" said Mr. Tonks, ruffling Jimmy's hair. "You just get on with your work in your best way and don't worry about Britomart. Things will come right, don't fret."

Jimmy went red with pleasure to hear Mr. Tonks's kind words. He smiled at the little elephant-man and went away, comforted. But almost at once he met Lotta running round a van. They bumped into one another, and Lotta laughed.

For a moment Jimmy wanted to laugh too. Then he remembered that Lotta had played him that mean trick and got him into trouble, and he didn't laugh. He turned away in silence.

"Jimmy!" cried Lotta. "What's the matter? Are you cross because I play with Lisa and Jeanne? I'll come for a walk with you and the dogs this morning, if you like."

"No, thank you," said Jimmy. "I expect you only say that because the two girls have gone down into the town, and you just happen to have nothing to do. I don't like girls—they play mean tricks."

Lotta didn't know what he meant. She stared after him. "*I* don't play mean tricks!" she cried.

"Oh yes, you do," said Jimmy, and he went off with his head in the air. Lotta tossed her own head and ran off angrily. All right—Jimmy could be horrid if he liked. *She* didn't care!

She went to Madame Prunella. Prunella was putting her parrots through their usual practice. One of them was saying, "Pop goes the weasel" very solemnly.

> "Half a pound of tuppenny rice,
> Half a pound of treacle,
> Stir it up and make it nice,
> POP goes the weasel!"

At the word POP all the other parrots joined in, and Gringle cackled with laughter. Lotta laughed too. She poked Sally, a big parrot, and whispered, "Britomart," to her.

Sally at once began the naughty little rhyme that Prunella had taught her:

> "Britomart
> Thinks he's smart,
> But he's got a stony heart!"

Neither of them saw that Britomart himself was nearby. The conjurer heard what the parrot shouted, and turned when he caught his own name. The parrot repeated the rhyme at the top of its voice, and then screeched with laughter.

Britomart strode over to the caravan. Lotta was stroking the parrot and tickling it. "Say it again, Sally," she said. "Say it again."

Then she looked up and saw Britomart standing nearby, his black eyes cold and angry. Sally began the rhyme again, her crested head cocked wickedly on one side.

"Hush!" said Lotta, and she nudged Madame Prunella to make her see who was standing near. Prunella looked up—but she didn't care tuppence for Britomart. He opened his mouth and began to speak, coldly and angrily.

At a little sign from their mistress the parrots set up their great screeching and squealing again, to drown the ring-master's deep voice. But this time Britomart was not to be beaten. He knew that it was no use trying to stop the parrots' noise—so he took firm hold of Madame Prunella's fat little arm, and made her come with him to where he could talk and be heard.

Prunella tried to shake off his hard fingers, but it was no use. Britomart was so strong that he could have lifted her up with one of his fingers and thumb.

"That parrot of yours will repeat his rhyme in the ring one night, Madame Prunella," said the ring-master. "And then, Madame, that will be the end of him."

"How dare you take hold of me in this way!" squealed Madame Prunella, flying into a temper at once. "Let go my arm. How dare you threaten one of my parrots!"

"That parrot will stay on its perch, and will not go into the ring, Madame Prunella," said Britomart. "I don't trust you. You have only to lose your temper in the ring one night to have all your parrots shouting stupid things about me. Now go back to your caravan and think over what I have said. That parrot does not go into the ring again!"

He let Prunella go, and the angry little woman shook her fist at Britomart's back, and screeched like a parrot.

"Sally's one of my best birds. She *shall* go into the ring—yes, and she shall sing many things about Britomart the conjurer."

She went back to her parrots, tears pouring down her cheeks, her hair standing on end. Lotta was waiting, wondering what Prunella was going to do.

"Madame Prunella," began Lotta, meaning to say that she was sorry she had made Sally begin the rhyme about Britomart without seeing if he was nearby. But Prunella would not let her say a word. When she was angry, she was angry with every one, friend or enemy alike. She glared at the little girl, and shouted at her.

"Go away! Pestering me like this! Go away!" She picked up her broom and began to sweep at Lotta. The little girl nearly fell over. She took one look at Prunella's angry red face, and ran off at top speed.

"Sausages and SMASH!" yelled Gringle after her.

"Well, there's plenty of 'smash' about," thought Lotta, as she heard things crashing behind her, when Prunella's broom knocked over pails and boxes. "Gringle's right! Goodness! It looks as if Madame Prunella's going to sweep up the whole circus!"

But after a time Prunella became quieter and took all her parrots into the cage. She meant to teach them something that would give Britomart a shock.

"The whole circus can be afraid of Britomart for all I care!" said Prunella. "*I'm* not afraid of him—and I'll soon show him what I can do!"

MORE TROUBLE!

ALTHOUGH all these upsets and quarrels went on in the camp, the show itself was splendid every night, for Britomart was a fine ring-master. The circus-folk knew that there was plenty of money coming in, and they were pleased about this. Pierre, the seal-trainer, was especially pleased, for he had not been lucky for some time.

So he chatted amiably with Britomart and praised the way he did things. Mrs. Pierre kept the conjurer's caravan clean for him, and the two girls, Lisa and Jeanne, went to help too. Not that they did anything much in the way of work, but they loved to try and peep at some of the things he used in his magic tricks.

"Look!" said Lisa, one morning. "Here's his magic black wand, Jeanne! It has rolled under this chest. Let's borrow it for a bit and see if we can do tricks with it."

The two girls smuggled it into their own caravan. But although they did their best with it, it did no tricks for them. They showed it to Lotta, and her eyes grew wide as she looked at Britomart's strange wand.

"Oooh!" she said. "However did you dare to take that? You'd better put it back."

"You try to do some tricks with it," said Lisa, putting it into the little girl's hands. "See if canaries come flying through the air, or goldfish swimming out of the ground!"

Just as Lotta was waving it in the air, Pierre came along. "Hide it, quick!" said Jeanne. "We shall get into trouble if our father knows we took that."

Lotta slipped the wand down the front of her frock and went to her own caravan with it. She put it under her mattress, meaning to try and see if she could do magic tricks with it later on. She knew that it was time for her to go and practise in the ring with Jimmy.

She and Jimmy hadn't made up their quarrel. Lotta was obstinate, and Jimmy was still hurt because he thought it was Lotta who had unlocked the seal's door and let the animal out after him.

"I shan't be nice again to Lotta till she owns up about that mean trick and says she's sorry," thought the boy to himself.

But as Lotta hadn't played the mean trick and didn't even know that Jimmy thought she had, she couldn't possibly own up to it! So things went on just as badly as before, and Lotta grew spiteful and rude, and Jimmy quiet and angry. It was all very horrid indeed.

That evening in the ring there was trouble—over Madame Prunella's parrots, of course. That angry little woman had spent two days teaching them a few new things!

She took Sally into the ring although Britomart had forbidden her to—and of course, Sally began her usual loud song of "Britomart, thinks he's smart" much to the ring-master's rage.

He cut Prunella's turn short, and ordered her out of the ring—but Prunella loosed all her parrots at once and they flew around the ring-master, screeching and squealing:

"Horrid Britomart!"

"Silly Britomart!"

"Get your moustaches cut! Get your moustaches cut!" (That was Sally, who learnt anything after hearing it said two or three times!)

"Poor old Britomart—poor old Britomart!" screeched another parrot in a doleful voice.

Of course, all the people thought that this was part of the show, and they roared with laughter. How they laughed and clapped! But Britomart was not pleased at all. He cracked his whip about the ring, and gave the parrots a fright. One of the things that the ring-master hated more than anything else in the world was to be laughed at, and he was very angry indeed now.

Prunella was afraid that he might hurt one of her parrots with the whip and she called them to her. They fluttered down to her arms and shoulders and head, and grinning cheekily, she bowed to all the clapping people. Her act was cut short—but she had got more claps than usual, all the same!

Britomart followed her out of the ring. "You will be sorry for this," he said in a furious voice. "I will see you to-morrow morning."

Prunella laughed. She skipped off with her parrots, and fetched her cloak. Lotta was standing nearby, waiting her turn to go into the ring with Black Beauty.

"That was fun, Madame Prunella!" she whispered. "Weren't your parrots naughty!"

But the other circus-folk looked rather grave. They felt certain that Britomart would punish Prunella in some way, and then things would be worse than ever.

Britomart had missed his black wand that evening, and had hunted everywhere for it. He called Mrs. Pierre to him about it.

"Did Lisa and Jeanne help you clean my caravan to-day?" he asked. "They did? Well, call them here. They may have seen my black wand."

The two girls came, rather scared. Britomart looked at them and saw at once that they had guilty faces. They knew something about his wand.

"You found my wand this morning, didn't you?" he said. "Bad girls! What did you do with it?"

Lisa was always quick at telling untruths to get herself out of trouble, so she answered in a hurry:

"Oh, Mr. Britomart, we did find it. It was under the chest there, but Lotta snatched it from us and took it away to see if it would do tricks for her. She wouldn't give it back though we told her to."

"So!" said Britomart, frowning, till his big black eyebrows met over his nose. "Lotta again! Tell her to come to me."

But Lotta had gone down into the town with her mother, and it was almost time for the show to begin when they came back. So she didn't know anything about the story

111

that naughty Lisa had told about her. She had forgotten about the wand too—it was still under her mattress! She had meant to put it back in Britomart's caravan and had quite forgotten.

She couldn't think why the ring-master looked at her so frowningly as she did her turn on Black Beauty that night. The pony was as clever as ever, and the little girl loved to feel his shiny black body beneath her, as she stood on him, sat, and knelt—even crawling right under his body as he galloped round and round the ring!

When the show was over she ran to look for Jimmy. "I say, Jimmy," she said, "do you think poor Madame Prunella will get into dreadful trouble to-morrow? What do you think Britomart will do? Will he send her away? Will he forbid her to go into the ring? Will he not pay her any money at all?"

Jimmy forgot that he wasn't friends with Lotta, and the two children stared at one another solemnly in the glaring lights that shone over the circus-field. They both liked Madame Prunella, and did not want anything horrid to happen to her.

"I don't know what Britomart will do," said Jimmy at last. "Anyway, all I know is this—I certainly don't want to get into trouble with him. Mr. Gilliano had a temper, but Britomart is far worse. Mr. Gilliano got into a temper, blew up, and forgot about it at once—but Britomart remembers always. That's why he never smiles, I expect—because he is always remembering horrid things!"

"Did you see how angrily he looked at me this evening?" asked Lotta. "I wondered what I'd done. I can't think of anything at all!"

Mrs. Brown called Jimmy, and he ran off with Lucky. He too had noticed Britomart watching Lotta angrily, and he had wondered why.

Jimmy and Lotta both lay awake that night and thought about Madame Prunella. They liked the excitable little woman very much, and neither of them liked to think of her in trouble. They felt sure that Britomart would send for her first thing in the morning.

And so he did. He called Pierre to him and gave him
112

an order. "Tell Madame Prunella I want her here in my caravan AT ONCE," he said in his deepest voice.

"Very good, sir," said Pierre, and went to tell Prunella.

But he couldn't find her caravan! It wasn't in its usual place. Pierre scratched his head and looked puzzled. Why had Prunella left her usual place? He looked round the enormous field, full of vans and carts and cages, and tried to see where Prunella had gone to.

He wandered round, looking for her gay caravan. He called Jimmy to him. "Have you seen Madame Prunella's caravan this morning?" he asked.

"No," said Jimmy, surprised. "Why, isn't it where it usually is, over by the stream?"

"No, she's moved it," said Pierre. "Oh my, there's Britomart yelling for me. Look round for Madame Prunella, there's a good boy, and tell her she's to go to Britomart AT ONCE!"

Britomart was impatiently waiting for Pierre. "What are you wandering all round the field for?" he said. "Where is Madame Prunella?"

"She seems to have moved her caravan, sir," said Pierre. "I was just looking for it."

Britomart made an angry noise and went down his caravan steps. He gazed round. He knew every van, cart, and cage.

"I can't see her caravan," he said at last. Then Jimmy came running up. "Please, sir, Madame Prunella isn't in the camp at all! Her caravan is gone! There are wheelmarks, new ones, going out of the gate! She must have put in her horse by herself last night, and stolen out quietly whilst we all slept."

"Pah!" said Britomart in anger. "How dare she leave my circus like that! She is part of the show. She has no right to do that without warning me. I shall see that she does not easily get a job in a circus again."

He went into the caravan and slammed the door. Jimmy was upset. It was horrid to think of pretty little Madame Prunella stealing off all alone in the night like that. How they would miss her and her screeching parrots!

113

But just then Britomart flung opon his door again. He had remembered his missing wand.

"Where's Lotta?" he called.

"In her caravan, sir," said Jimmy in surprise. "Why, do you want her?"

"Yes—I want her—and I want something else, too!" said Britomart in a grim voice. And he strode over the field to Lotta's caravan. What a shock poor Lotta was going to get!

BRITOMART tapped on the door of Lotta's caravan. Rat-tat-tat! Lotta opened the door in surprise, for not many people knocked like that. When she saw Britomart standing there, frowning, she was even more astonished.

"Lotta, you have my black wand, I think," said the ring-master in his deep voice. Lotta stared at him in dismay. She had forgotten all about the wand. She went very red indeed.

"Where is it?" said Britomart. He pushed his way into the caravan, and looked round. Lotta went to her bunk, felt about under the mattress, and gave it to Britomart, trembling, for he looked so angry.

"How dare you go to my caravan and steal my wand!" thundered the ring-master. "I always said that children should never be allowed in any circus. You are a bad little girl."

Lotta didn't know what to say. She didn't like to say that Lisa had taken the wand and lent it to her, in case she got Lisa into trouble too. She did not know that Lisa had told a bad untruth, and put the whole blame on Lotta. So the little girl stood there and said nothing at all, looking frightened and sulky.

But Jimmy, who was listening, called out in alarm, "Mr. Britomart! I'm sure Lotta didn't steal your wand. She wouldn't steal anything. She——"

"Hold your tongue, boy," ordered the ring-master. "I am not speaking to you, but to this naughty girl. Lotta, I will not have you in the ring for two weeks! You can stay out, and see how you like that. Lisa and Jeanne can take your place. They do not ride so well as you, but they are good

115

enough. Perhaps that will teach you to leave other people's things alone in future."

Britomart turned and went down the steps. He pushed Jimmy roughly aside and went to his own caravan with his wand, a tall and stern figure. Jimmy did not dare to say anything more to him. He was afraid that if he did he too might be forbidden to go into the ring.

He was dreadfully sorry for Lotta. The little girl stood in the middle of her caravan as if she was turned into stone. She did not move or say a word. Jimmy ran up the steps to her, meaning to comfort her, forgetting all about the mean trick he thought she played on him.

But Lotta pushed him away. She pushed him right down the steps, slammed the caravan door and locked it. She even shut the windows and drew the curtains across. Jimmy was quite shut out. He heard Lotta fling herself down on her untidy bunk, and begin to sob. Poor Jimmy! It was dreadful to feel so sorry for some one and not to be able to help them. He went away after a time, and hunted for Lal, Lotta's mother.

He told her all that had happened. Lal was angry and worried.

"Poor Lotta," she said. "I'm sure she didn't take that wand from Britomart's caravan. I feel certain Lisa or Jeanne have had something to do with this, horrid little creatures!"

"You'd better go to Lotta," said Jimmy anxiously. "She's awfully unhappy. You know how proud she is of going into the ring with Black Beauty each night, and how she loves sharing my turn with Lucky. Now Lisa and Jeanne are going to ride instead. But I won't let them share my turn with little dog Lucky."

Lal went off to try and comfort Lotta. But the miserable little girl wouldn't even unlock the door. She lay and wept till she had no tears left, thinking of the time when dear old Mr. Galliano ran the circus, and everything went right. She couldn't bear Britomart. She couldn't bear Lisa and Jeanne now, either, because they were going into the ring instead of her. Oh! Oh! How she hated every one!

"Better leave her alone to get over it," said Mrs. Brown,

when Lal told her what had happened. "You know, Lal, this may do Lotta good. She hasn't been a very nice child lately, and she has rather got into the habit of thinking that she can do just whatever she likes. She is a good little girl at heart—but she has been very naughty lately."

"Perhaps you're right," said Lal, thinking of the rude faces and cheeky answers that Lotta had given her. "Maybe all the clapping and cheering she gets each night has made her vain."

"Oh, how horrid you both are to talk of poor Lotta like that!" said Jimmy, who was very tender-hearted. "She's terribly unhappy now, I know she is—and I don't care whether she deserves it or not, I'm sorry for her and I'd put things right if I could. I'd like to swing Britomart's whip round his great long legs!"

"Hush, Jimmy, don't talk like that," said his mother, shocked. "If Britomart hears you, he will forbid you to go into the ring too—and then you will not get paid and will have to go without a good many of the nice things you like so much."

Jimmy stamped his foot and went off by himself. He was angry, miserable, and puzzled. He couldn't believe that Lotta had stolen Britomart's wand. But if she hadn't, how was it that it was in her caravan? Jimmy didn't know. He only knew that things were queer and horrid lately.

Lisa and Jeanne were excited and pleased when they heard that they were to ride in the ring instead of Lotta. They did not feel sorry for their friend. They were glad because they were going to take her place. They were hard, selfish little girls, vain and bold. They danced round in excitement when their mother fitted them for their circus-dresses.

"Lisa can borrow Lotta's," said Britomart. "They are much of a size. Perhaps Lal has an old dress of Lotta's that she has grown out of, that would do for Jeanne. There is no time to make new ones."

So, much to Lotta's anger, Lisa and Jeanne put on her own dresses, the pretty, sparkling ones that made her like a fairy. Lisa and Jeanne looked lovely in them too, for they were both pretty children, with their red curls and snub noses. It made Lotta more unhappy to think of Lisa and Jeanne wearing her dresses than she felt when she thought of them taking her place in the ring that night.

"But they shan't ride Black Beauty," she told her mother furiously. "They shan't! If they do, I'll get on Black Beauty's back and ride right away and never come back, Lal!"

"Don't be silly, Lotta," said Lal. "Of course no one will ride Black Beauty. He is in his stable, quite happy."

But Black Beauty was not happy. He knew that his little mistress was sad, and he was sad too. He could not understand why she did not come to get him ready for the night's show. He stamped impatiently in his stable but Lotta did not come.

Black Beauty whinnied, and Lotta heard him. She had refused to go out of her caravan all that day, but she could not say no when Black Beauty called her. She slipped out when no one was looking and went to his stable. He rubbed his black nose against her lovingly and the little girl threw her arms round his neck.

"Oh, Black Beauty, we're not going into the ring tonight," she sobbed. "It's not fair that you should be punished too, because you do love showing how well you can dance and do tricks, don't you? But nobody shall ride you if *I* can't. We'll have to let that silly Lisa and stupid Jeanne take our places."

At that moment Lisa and Jeanne came running by, dressed in Lotta's pretty clothes. They saw Lotta and called to her.

"Hallo, Lotta! So you've come out at last! Look at us—aren't we fine? We're going to do as well as we can, so that Britomart will perhaps let us be in the circus always."

Lotta turned away without a word. She wondered how she could ever have liked Lisa and Jeanne—how she could have played with them and been so unkind to Jimmy, who had been her friend for so long. She would never, never play with them again.

Then she thought of something and turned round on Lisa. "How did Britomart know that I had his wand?" she demanded. "Did you tell him?"

Lisa looked at Jeanne and Jeanne looked at Lisa. They had both made up their minds what to say if Lotta asked them that question.

"What do you mean?" asked Lisa, with an innocent wide-eyed stare. "Of course we didn't tell him. We didn't even know you had it."

"Oh, you dreadful fibber!" cried Lotta. "Why, you gave it to me yourself, Lisa, when you had found it under the chest!"

"We didn't find it under any chest," said Jeanne, bounding off. "*You* found it, and you must have taken it without anyone knowing."

Lotta stared after the two mean, untruthful girls in amazement. For a moment she couldn't imagine what they meant. And then she guessed everything.

"They must have told Britomart that *I* took the wand from his caravan," she cried. "Oh, the fibbers! I'll go and tell him straightaway that I didn't."

Off she rushed to Britomart's caravan. She thumped on the door.

"Go away!" ordered Britomart, who was busy changing into his circus-dress. "I see no one now."

"Mr. Britomart! It's me, Lotta!" cried the little girl. "I've come to tell you that Lisa told you a story about me. *She* took your wand, not me—she gave it to me to see if I could do any tricks with it, and——"

"Go away," said Britomart. "I do not believe you. You are a naughty girl, disobedient and sulky. Go away."

So that wasn't any good either. Lotta went away, tears in her eyes. She met Oona the acrobat in his sparkling tights, ready for the ring. He looked solemn.

"Have you heard anything about Madame Prunella?" asked Lotta, remembering that Prunella was Oona's cousin and that the acrobat was very fond of her. Oona shook his head.

"No," he said sadly. "I am unhappy about Prunella. It is the first time she has ever run away from a show—and it is not good to do that. No ring-master likes to take people who have run away from shows, in case it might happen again—and that harms a circus, you know. Britomart

119

always rubs people up the wrong way. I don't think I shall stay on with the circus when we leave here."

"Oh, Oona, don't say that!" cried Lotta. "The circus wouldn't be the same without you."

Oona wasn't the only one thinking about leaving. Mr. Wally was gloomily planning to take Sammy to another show if Gilliano didn't come back soon. And if Mr. Wally went, then Mr. Tonks declared he would go to.

"Why, there won't be any of Mr. Gilliano's Circus left!" thought Lotta miserably. "Whatever are we to do?"

WHAT WILL HAPPEN TO THE CIRCUS?

IT seemed strange without Madame Prunella, and every one missed the noise of the screeching parrots. Nobody knew where Prunella had gone. Nobody heard from her. It was very mysterious. Britomart did not mention her name, but he altered the turns in the ring to make up for Madame Prunella's turn being missed out.

Pierre got an even longer turn, and so did Google the clown. Twinkle, Pippi, and Stanley were annoyed about this, because they thought they should have more time given to them.

Sticky Stanley asked Britomart if he and the other two might not have five minutes more. Britomart shook his head.

"Google is funnier than you three," he said. "You do not get so many laughs as he does—he shall have the extra time. And please do not question what I do—I am the ring-master and my word is law."

Sharp-faced Google was pleased. A longer turn meant more money. He went across the field to talk to Pierre, who was also pleased that his own turn was to be longer, Squib, Google's dog, went at his heels.

He saw Lucky on the way and stopped to talk to him. He was very good friends with Lucky. Jimmy saw them playing together as he came up with biscuits for Lucky, and he threw one to Squib.

Google saw him and swung round. "Don't feed my dog!" he ordered. "You children think you can do what you like in this circus. Squib! Come here!"

Squib did not want to come, with that beautiful smell of biscuit just under his nose. He stood there, wagging his tail, looking towards his master as if to say, "Please, Master, just let me wait and have a nibble, then I'll come."

Google was always jealous if Squib liked anyone else, and he was furious because his dog would not leave Jimmy and Lucky, and come to him. He strode over to them, picked Squib up, and tried to cuff Jimmy. The boy slipped out of the way, his eyes shining with rage.

Google went off, muttering.

"That's the first time anyone has tried to cuff me in this circus," thought Jimmy. "Lotta's right. This isn't Mr. Galliano's circus any longer. It's Britomart's—and it's getting like him—quarrelsome, selfish, hard, and horrid!"

For the first time a thought came into the boy's mind. If Mr. Wally went—and Mr. Tonks and Jumbo went— why shouldn't he go too? Why shouldn't he go with them, and join another circus, where perhaps there would be a nicer ring-master than Britomart? His mother and father could go with him, for any circus would be glad of Brownie's help as carpenter and handyman.

"And I guess you and I could get a job in another circus as easily as anything!" said Jimmy, stroking Lucky's soft head. "I don't believe old Galliano will ever come back— and I'm not going to work for Britomart much longer! He has never once said how clever you are, Lucky. He looks at us as if we are worms. We won't stand it, will we?"

"Woof, woof!" said Lucky, lying on her back with all four paws in the air. She would go anywhere with Jimmy and be happy.

"You see, Lucky, even Lotta doesn't seem the same," said Jimmy, tickling Lucky. "We've had such fun together, she and I, and Black Beauty and you—but now she mustn't go into the ring, and she's cross and miserable and won't be friends. So perhaps it would be better to go right away, Lucky, and start all over again."

Lisa and Jeanne came chattering by. They were very pleased at going into the ring each night. They were a great success, for although they were not nearly so clever as Lotta, they could both ride well, and looked pretty in the ring.

Lisa pulled Jimmy's hair as she passed. "You look as if you're going to burst into tears!" she said. "Cheer up!"

Jimmy turned his back on her. "I suppose you think you do marvellously in the ring!" he said. "But, my goodness, what a pair of scarecrows you look! You ought to be ashamed of yourselves, doing poor old Lotta out of her turn. I thought you were supposed to be friends of hers."

"My word, isn't he a bear!" laughed Jeanne, and the two girls danced off happily, very pleased with themselves these days. Things were going right with them!

Jimmy went into the ring after a while to give Lucky a practice. Mr. Wally was there with Sammy the chimpanzee, giving him a practice too.

Mr. Wally was looking worried. Sammy was not behaving well. He was sulky. He was supposed to undress himself in the ring and put himself to bed in a cot, which he usually did very well indeed. But to-day he sat on the floor and moped, and although Mr. Wally did his best to coax him, he hung his hairy head and would not do anything to please his master.

When he saw Jimmy coming in with Lucky he leapt to his feet and made chattering noises of joy. He ran to Jimmy and put his arms round the boy's waist, nearly lifting him off the ground with delight.

"Oh, Sammy! Dear old Sammy!" said Jimmy. "Look, Mr. Wally, he's even trying to kiss me!"

"He's so pleased to see you," said Mr. Wally. "You know, Jimmy, he's moping terribly, now that he is not allowed to wander about with me and you as he likes. And since you've been forbidden to play with him in his cage each day he is worse than ever. Chimpanzees are like children, you know—they must have plenty to do and see, or they mope, and get miserable. Now, Sammy—will you do your tricks for Jimmy?"

Oh, yes! Sammy didn't mind doing them for his beloved friend Jimmy. The chimpanzee went through his tricks happily, laughing when Jimmy clapped him. His queer chimpanzee mind had not been able to understand why his friend hadn't been to see him—and he couldn't think why nobody took him for walks round the field now.

Jimmy took Sammy's paw and led him back to his cage when his practice was over. They met Britomart on the way, and then the ring-master saw Jimmy with the chimpanzee, he frowned.

"Didn't I say that you were not to play with the animals any more?" he demanded. "Mr. Wally, you know my orders, even if Jimmy doesn't!"

Mr. Wally had a temper of his own. He flared up at once.

"Mr. Britomart," he said, "every one in this circus knows your orders. We can't help knowing them. You throw them at our heads all day long. We have had more orders from you in a few weeks than we had from Mr. Galliano in a year! But I'm not aware that either I or Jimmy are disobeying your orders at the moment. Jimmy is not playing with Sammy. He is merely walking back to his cage with him."

"That is enough from you, Mr. Wally," said the ring-master in anger.

"No, it isn't enough," said Mr. Wally. "Not nearly enough! My chimpanzee is moping, Mr. Britomart, because of your orders. He won't do his tricks properly! If Jimmy hadn't come into the ring this morning, Sammy wouldn't have done a single one of his tricks. No animal can perform if it mopes!"

"I thought your chimpanzee was not doing so well this week," said Mr. Britomart coldly. "I had thought I would get some one else in his place, when we leave this camp."

"That suits me all right," said Mr. Wally, going very red indeed. "In fact, that suits me fine! I'm not staying in any circus with you, Mr. Britomart. And let me tell you this—the whole circus will break up if you go about shouting orders at us from morning to night! Why, you are spoiling the very things you ought to use! Look at this boy, Jimmy, here—he keeps all the animals happy—they all love him—and what do you do but forbid him to play with them! Pah!"

"I shall listen to you no longer," said Britomart, white with anger. He turned and walked off. But Mr. Wally hadn't finished with him yet.

"And what about little Lotta?" he yelled. "You go and

JIMMY TOOK SAMMY'S PAW AND LED HIM BACK TO THE CAGE

shut her out of the ring and put in those two silly red-haired kids instead. They can't ride for toffee! They . . ."

But Britomart was out of hearing. Sammy the chimpanzee suddenly began to whimper. He knew that Mr. Wally was angry and he did not like it. He was frightened. Jimmy put his arm round the chimpanzee and hugged him.

"It's all right, Sammy," he said. "Mr. Wally is just telling Mr. Britomart a few things he ought to know. Good for you, Mr. Wally! But, I say—you won't really go, will you?"

"I certainly will," said Mr. Wally in a most determined voice. "And what's more, I'll take old Tonks with me, and Volla too, and Stanley and Lilliput! If anyone thinks I'm going to put up with Britomart, they're mistaken!"

And off he marched to put Sammy into his cage. Jimmy watched him with a sinking heart. It seemed as if the circus would break up before his very eyes!

"I'll have to go too," he thought. "I can't possibly stay here without all my friends."

He went off, thinking hard. "I shan't tell Lotta I'm going," he thought. "She won't care anyhow! So she shan't hear any of my plans from *me!*"

JIMMY LEARNS THE TRUTH

LOTTA was very miserable now. She hated to think of Lisa and Jeanne going in the ring to take her place each night. She would not speak to the two girls, nor would she speak to Jimmy. She just moped about the field, sometimes riding Black Beauty to give him the exercise he needed.

Jimmy did his turn with Lucky in the ring, but he would not let Lisa and Jeanne help him. The two girls begged and begged him to let them, but Jimmy shook his head.

"No," he said, "you are both mean and horrid. I won't have you helping me with Lucky in the ring And if you dare to ask Britomart if you can, I'll walk right out of this circus like Madame Prunella!"

He looked so fierce that the two girls said no more. Neither of them would have dared to ask anything from Britomart, for cheeky as they were, they were just as much afraid of the stern ring-master as anyone else was.

But Jeanne, the younger girl, wouldn't give up trying to make friends with Jimmy. She had suddenly decided that if only she could make Jimmy really friendly with her, he might let her, and not Lisa, go into the ring with him and Lucky. "Then wouldn't Lisa be jealous!" she thought.

So Jeanne began to be very nice to Jimmy. She brought him a hot chocolate-cake that her mother had just made. But all that Jimmy said was—"Hmmm! I suppose you took that when your mother's back was turned. I don't want any, thank you! I think you and Lisa are untruthful, dishonest girls."

"Oh, Jimmy! Don't be so unkind!" said Jeanne. "I know Lisa is horrid and unkind often—but I'm quite different. I don't tell dreadful fibs like Lisa."

"Well, *I've* never noticed that you were any better than

Lisa," said Jimmy, polishing some horse harness so hard that his arm ached. "Anyway, I don't like you, so go away."

Jeanne squeezed a few tears out and sniffed dolefully. "Well, Jimmy," she said. "I was very sorry that Lisa told that dreadful story the other day—you know, about letting Neptune out."

"What do you mean?" asked Jimmy in surprise. "What dreadful story?"

"Why, don't you remember? Lisa said that Lotta had unlocked the door of the seal's van, so that Neptune might go after you, and then you'd get into trouble," said Jeanne. "Well, it wasn't Lotta. Lotta said she wouldn't play a mean trick like that. But Lisa did, and then she said it was Lotta who had done it."

Jimmy stared at Jeanne in the greatest surprise and anger. *Lisa* had played the trick—and had blamed Lotta for it! The horrid girl!

"If I could get hold of Lisa, I'd pull her red hair till she yelled the place down!" said the boy furiously. "It was Lisa who got me into trouble over the seal, then, and not poor old Lotta—and here I've been blaming Lotta for it, and thinking horrid things about her—and they weren't a bit true! Oh, I do feel mean!"

"Yes, and Lisa got Lotta into trouble too," said tell-tale Jeanne, thoroughly enjoying herself. "It was Lisa who gave Lotta the wand to hide, and who told Britomart that Lotta had found it and taken it."

Jimmy simply couldn't believe his ears. He couldn't think that anyone could be so horrid. He stood and stared at Jeanne till that bold little girl began to feel uncomfortable.

"I've only told you all this, Jimmy, because I want to show you I'd like to be friends," she said.

"You've told tales of your sister, you've shown me exactly how mean and nasty you both are—and then you say it's to show me you want to be friends," said Jimmy at last in a disgusted voice. "Well, listen to me, Jeanne— you and Lisa have made a lot of trouble and mischief, but it's the last time you do it to me or to Lotta. I don't want

128

to have anything more to do with you. I don't want to speak to you. I don't want to look at you. I won't even work in the same circus as you! After we leave here I shall join another circus—and I hope I never meet either you or Lisa again!"

The angry boy turned on his heel and went away, taking the jingling harness with him. Jeanne stared after him, red in the face. For the first time in her life she felt ashamed of herself. Perhaps after all it was a better thing to tell the truth, to be honest and loyal and kind, like Jimmy. Jeanne began to cry, and wished that she hadn't told tales.

Jimmy hung up the harness in the stable-van and went off by himself. He wanted to think. Lucky ran silently at her master's heels, knowing that he was worried. Together they went off over the fields, and when Jimmy found a sweet-scented gorse-bush throwing its delicious smell over a common, he sat down by it.

Lucky lay down by him, her head on Jimmy's knees. Jimmy stroked the soft head. "You know, Lucky," he said, "I've been unfair to poor old Lotta. I thought she had played me that mean trick, and let Neptune out to get me into trouble—but I might have known Lotta would never do a thing like that, little monkey though she is."

"Woof," said Lucky softly. She loved Jimmy to talk to her like this. She put out her pink tongue and licked her master's brown hand.

"And Lotta's got into dreadful trouble all because of Lisa, too," said Jimmy. "She's very unhappy. And she must be puzzled to know why I've been so extra horrid to her. So we've got to put things straight, Lucky. Haven't we?"

"Woof, woof!" said Lucky, quite agreeing.

"Well, the first thing we'll do, Lucky, is to go down into the town and buy Lotta the biggest and best doll we can find," said Jimmy. "She loves dolls, you know, and she's never had one of her own. Perhaps that will make her feel happier. And then, Lucky, we'll tell her that everything has been a silly, horrid mistake, and we'll all be friends again. What do you think of that idea?"

"WOOF!" said Lucky, sitting up. It was plain that she thought it a very good idea indeed!

"You're a marvellous dog," said Jimmy, hugging Lucky. "I believe you understand every single word I say! I really do. And, Lucky, we'll wait and see what Mr. Galliano's next letter says, shall we—and if he is coming back soon we'll stay here—and if he's not, we'll give Britomart notice that we are both going off to another circus. Lotta must come too. Things will soon be better, once we make up our minds to face them and see how we can beat the things we don't like!"

Lucky bounded round, her eyes shining, as she heard her master's determined voice. She knew quite well that Jimmy had made up his mind about something and was feeling happier. Then little dog Lucky was happy too!

The two went back to the camp. Jimmy looked about for Lotta, but the little girl was nowhere to be seen.

"Well, never mind, I'll go down to the town now and buy that doll," said Jimmy. "It's funny that girls like things like dolls—but they all seem to, even Lotta. So maybe they can't help it. Come on, Lucky!"

Jimmy took some money from his money-box and went off with his dog at his heels. He couldn't help feeling much happier now that he knew it was Lisa who had got him into trouble and not Lotta. He caught a tram and was soon in the heart of the big town.

He looked about for a toy-shop. He soon found one— a rather marvellous one, with all kinds of toys in it, from bears to rabbits, dolls to trains, bricks to scooters, cars to books—everything that could be thought of! Jimmy gazed in at the window.

He looked at the dolls carefully. There were all kinds. There was a baby-doll dressed in long clothes, whose eyes shut, and who had tiny shining nails like a real baby. There was a cheeky-looking doll dressed in a coat and hat —but it had red hair and reminded Jimmy of Lisa and Jeanne. He couldn't possibly have *that* doll!

There were airmen-dolls, soldier-dolls, and sailor-dolls —but Jimmy didn't feel that they were the kind of dolls that Lotta would like. And then he saw the Very Doll! It was sitting in a little chair, and had a sweet smiling face, with bright blue eyes, tiny teeth, and red cheeks. Its hair was real, and fell in golden curls.

Jimmy stared at the doll. He couldn't help rather liking it himself, it was such a friendly, smiling doll. It was dressed in a gay overall, and beside it were a red hat and coat, ready to put on—and a little red umbrella too!

"That's the doll for Lotta!" thought Jimmy. He looked at the price-ticket. It was very expensive—seventeen shillings and sixpence! Jimmy counted up his money. He could just buy it!

"Well, it's worth it, to make poor old Lotta a bit happy again," thought Jimmy, going into the shop. He pointed out the doll to the shop-girl and she took it out of the window. Jimmy took it and looked at it. The doll smiled up at him and almost seemed as if it was going to laugh.

"Put it into a box, please," said Jimmy, "and wrap it up nicely. It's for a present."

The girl wrapped up the doll and Jimmy paid her his money. He went out of the shop and caught the next tram back, out of the town. He walked down the country lane that led to the camp, whistling happily. It was a simply lovely feeling to carry a fine surprise like that under his arm, ready to give to someone who was miserable!

He got to the camp. "Lotta!" he yelled. "Lotta! Where are you?"

"She's in her caravan," said Oona. "I saw her going up the steps twenty minutes ago."

Jimmy went and banged on the door. "Lotta! Let me in. I've something to show you."

"Don't want to see it," said a sulky voice. But Jimmy wasn't going to take any notice of that. He flung open the caravan door and went in, beaming all over his brown face.

A FINE OLD MUDDLE!

LOTTA was alone in her caravan. She was untidy and dirty, for since Britomart had forbidden her to go into the ring, she had been too sulky and unhappy to care how she looked.

She spent a good deal of time shut up in her caravan, for she didn't like to meet Lisa and Jeanne in the camp. They were unkind, and loved to tell her how well they were getting on, riding in the ring each night. She didn't like to meet Jimmy either, for he too seemed more of an enemy than a friend these days. So the sad little girl shut herself up with Lulu the spaniel and thought back to all the happy days when Mr. Galliano had the circus.

"I know what I shall do," she decided. "I shall do what I did once before—dress up as a boy, cut my hair short, and run away. Nobody cares about me any more. Jimmy isn't my friend. Mrs. Brown says I am spoilt and rude. Even Lal tells me I deserve to be punished. So I shall run away from everybody—then perhaps they will be sorry."

It was whilst she was thinking this that Jimmy arrived and banged on the door. It flew open, and Lotta saw Jimmy standing there, a broad smile on his face—the first smile she had seen on Jimmy's face for quite a long time.

"Lotta! I've got a present for you," cried Jimmy.

"A present? What for? It isn't my birthday," said Lotta, surprised.

"I know that. It's a present to make up for being horrid to you, and thinking untrue things about you," said Jimmy. "Oh, Lotta—I thought *you* had opened Neptune's door and let him out after me to get me into trouble, and I thought it was simply horrid of you and I wouldn't be friends at all —and now Jeanne has told me it was Lisa who did it."

"Oh—the mean creature!" cried Lotta in a rage. "As if I'd play a trick like that on you, Jimmy. You might have known I'd never do a thing like that."

132

"Yes, I might have known it," said Jimmy. "I'm terribly sorry I was so horrid all for nothing, Lotta—just when things went wrong for you too. And I've found out that it was Lisa who got that wand, not you—and she gave it to you and told Britomart you had stolen it. But *I* never, never once thought that, Lotta. Really I didn't."

"I should just hope you didn't," cried Lotta, her eyes flashing. "Good gracious! To think that awful Lisa said things like that about me. I'll pull her hair out. I'll pinch her hard. I'll——"

"Well, before you do that, just take a look at this," said Jimmy, afraid that Lotta would fly out of the caravan to find Lisa that very minute. He pushed the big parcel into Lotta's hands. The little girl looked at it, and then began to tug eagerly at the string. Like all the circus-folk, she really loved a present.

The string came off. The paper slid to the floor. Lotta took off the lid of the box—and the blue-eyed, golden-haired doll smiled up at her in its friendly, loving way.

"*Jimmy!* A real doll of my own—and the loveliest, darlingest one too!" squealed Lotta in the greatest delight. "Jimmy, how did you think of such a present? Oh, Jimmy, I do love it. It's the most beautiful doll I ever saw—much, *much* nicer than Lisa's or Jeanne's. And oh, look at its overall—and its little red coat and hat—and gracious goodness, it's got an umbrella too!"

Jimmy stood and grinned all over his face at Lotta's delight. He had never felt so pleased in his life as when he saw Lotta's face at that moment. Lotta was his friend, and she had been unhappy, and now she was happy again. Jimmy felt warm and happy too.

"You give her a name, Jimmy," she said.

"Lisa," said Jimmy at once, with a grin.

Lotta squealed and made a face. "Don't be silly. I wouldn't give the name of a horrid girl to a lovely doll like this. I'll call her Rosemary Josephine Annabella—there, dolly, three beautiful names for you!"

Lotta put the doll back into its box and looked at Jimmy. She flung her arms round his neck and hugged him. "You've made me feel happy again," she said. "Let's be friends again, Jimmy. I'm awfully sorry I was horrid to you when I went to play with Lisa and Jeanne. I can't think how I behaved like that now."

"Well, we'll forgive one another and begin all over again," said Jimmy. "You know, Lotta, it's not been all our fault really—things have gone so badly since Mr. Galliano went away, and Britomart seems to have upset everything and everybody. Did you know that half the circus-folk are leaving after this show is ended?"

"No," said Lotta, startled. "I haven't talked to anybody, really, these last few days. Do you mean they're leaving Galliano's Circus—not coming back? I know Oona was thinking of it, but I didn't know all the others were too."

"Well, Mr. Wally's going," said Jimmy, and he told Lotta about the quarrel between Britomart and Mr. Wally. "And Mr. Volla's going—and Tonks—yes, and I'm going too, Lotta."

"Jimmy!" cried Lotta in dismay, clutching at his arm. "Don't say that! I couldn't stay here without you—oh, just think of having to live with Lisa and Jeanne always!"

"You needn't," said Jimmy. "You and Lal and Laddo must leave too. See, Lotta? We'll all leave together. We'll go and join another circus, and have a fine time, just as we always used to have."

"But supposing Mr. Galliano comes back?" asked Lotta. "He'd be very unhappy to find his circus split up."

"Well, we'll wait and see what his next letter says," promised Jimmy. "I won't tell Britomart I'm going until after we've heard from Mr. Galliano. Then we'll know what to do."

So it was left like that, and the children waited impatiently for more news of Galliano. Lotta was much happier now. She loved her doll, and spent hours dressing and undressing it. She was very sweet to Jimmy, and tried her best to be good and helpful to Mrs. Brown and Lal. They were pleased, and thought that the old nice little Lotta had come back once more.

Britomart at last had another letter from Mr. Galliano. The news went round the camp at once, for the postman gave the letter to Sticky Stanley to deliver to Britomart and the clown knew the writing at once. Every one gathered in a crowd outside Britomart's caravan to hear the news. Soon the ring-master appeared with the letter in his hand, his face as stern as ever.

"You seem to know that I have a letter from Mr. Galliano," he said, glancing round at every one. "You will wish to hear what he says. I will read it to you."

He unfolded the letter and read it.

"DEAR BRITOMART, AND DEAR FRIENDS ALL,—You will be happy to know that Mrs. Galliano is much better now, and in six months' time she will be as well as ever she was. She has to go for a long holiday now, in the south of France—and as the show is going so well under the direction of your new ring-master, I shall take a holiday and go with her. So I shall not be back with you for some time. I will write again as soon as I have news. I send my best wishes to you all, and hope that the show will go on doing as splendidly as ever.

"GALLIANO."

Google and Pierre were pleased, for they were the favourites of Britomart. But no one else looked pleased except Lisa and Jeanne. With whisperings and mutterings the rest of the circus-folk went back to their caravans sad at heart. Galliano wasn't coming back for half a year. They couldn't work for Britomart so long. It was impossible. The circus must break up.

That day Mr. Volla went to Britomart and warned him that he and his bears would leave the circus when the run was finished. Lilliput said the same. Mr. Tonks said the same too, but very sadly, for he had been with Mr. Galliano's circus for many years. Oona the acrobat said he was going, and Sticky Stanley the clown.

And Jimmy marched up the caravan steps, too, and told the ring-master that he and Lucky would find a new circus as soon as they left the show-place they were in. Jimmy's heart beat fast as he said this, for Britomart was angry and white.

"Go then," he said to Jimmy. "There are many dogs as clever as yours. We shall not miss you!"

Jimmy went to find Lotta. He told her that he had

warned Britomart that he and Lucky would soon be looking for another circus. He had already spoken about it to his mother and father, and they were quite willing to leave, and to go seeking a happier circus in their pretty blue-and-yellow caravan. They had plenty of money for a holiday first.

Lotta flew to find Lal and Laddo. "Lal! Laddo! Every one's leaving Britomart's circus. Have you told him we will go too? I won't stay! I won't!"

Lal and Laddo looked grave. Laddo shook his head. "We can't go, Lotta," he said. "We signed a paper to promise Britomart that we would stay with him for at least a year. We shall have to stay."

"Laddo!" cried Lotta in horror. "You don't mean we'll *have* to stay! You can't mean that! Why, everyone's going —even Jimmy! I can't be left behind if Jimmy's going!"

"You'll have to stay behind," said Lal. "The others only promised to stay till the end of this show, but Britomart made us promise to stay for a year. We promised for you too, Lotta. So you'll have to make the best of it."

"Oh! Oh!" wailed Lotta. "Everything's going wrong again! Oh, Lal! Let me go with Mrs. Brown and Jimmy, and you stay on here."

"Of course not, Lotta," said Laddo. "Don't be such a baby. We have to earn our living—and we are staying on with Britomart to earn it. He pays us well, and though we don't like him, it can't be helped. It's time you grew up a little and knew that you have often to do things you don't like."

Lotta fled away, sobbing. She found Jimmy and poured out her woes to him. Jimmy was horrified. "Oh, goodness, Lotta—I'd never, never have said I'd go if I'd thought you'd have to stay. I'll go and tell Britomart that I'll stay on!"

But that wasn't any good. Britomart was sharp and short with Jimmy. "Once you give me your notice and say you want to go, that finishes it," said Britomart in his cold, deep voice.

"Now here's a fine old muddle," thought Jimmy in dismay. "How in the world are we going to get out of it? *I* don't know."

LOTTA DISAPPEARS!

THE show was going to come to an end in a week's time. The circus had had a marvellous run, but it was now time to move on. As the circus-folk had made a great deal of money, most of them meant to have a holiday before joining another circus. But nobody felt very happy even about their holiday.

"It's so horrid to split up like this, just when we had such a good show together," said Lilliput, stroking Jemima, who was round his neck as usual—though on a lead now.

"But we can most of us meet in another circus," said Jimmy hopefully.

Lilliput shook his head. "Some of us may," he said, "but it rather depends on who is already in a circus, you know. For instance, *you* might be taken on with Mr. Phillippino's show, Jimmy, because he has no performing dogs at all at present, and he'd be glad to have you—but I wouldn't be taken on there because there is already a trainer with seven monkeys. Phillippino's wouldn't want two lots of monkeys."

"I see," said Jimmy, his heart sinking. "Oh, Lilliput—I shall so hate to say good-bye to any of my friends. As for leaving Lotta behind, I can't bear to think of it."

"Well, you'll have to, son," said Lilliput sadly. "That's the worst of the circus-world—there are such a lot of good-byes; but never mind, we usually meet again in the end."

"I never want to meet Lisa and Jeanne again," said Jimmy fiercely. "And they'll probably be the very ones I *shall* meet!"

Lilliput laughed. "Cheer up! Those youngsters will get themselves into trouble one day. I can see it coming."

When Lotta's two weeks were up, Britomart sent a message to Lal to say that Lotta might ride in the ring again that night. There was now hardly one more week left of the show, and he wanted the clever little girl to do her turn.

"Lal, what about Lisa and Jeanne?" asked Lotta. "They won't be riding in the ring, will they, if I do?"

"Yes," said Lal. "Their mother has made them frocks of their own, and Britomart says they may share your turn. They have done very well, Lotta. I don't like either of them, but they are quite clever with horses."

"If they are going to share my turn, I won't go into the ring," said Lotta, sticking out her round little chin in a determined manner.

"You'll have to, if Britomart says you are to," said Lal. "Don't be silly, Lotta. You are acting like a baby. It was your own fault that you were punished, after all."

"Well, it just wasn't!" said Lotta. "It was Lisa's fault. I didn't tell you before—but everything has been Lisa's fault, really it has, Lal. And it is a dreadful feeling to think I'll have to say on with Britomart's circus, and see that horrid Lisa every day!"

Lotta was nearly in tears. Lal was very sorry for the little girl, but she couldn't see that things could be altered. Lal knew very well that it was impossible to have everything as one liked it—sometimes things went well and sometimes they went badly. Well, people just had to put up with whatever happened, and show a brave face and laugh, that was all!

"Mrs. Brown has washed and ironed your circus-frock," she said. "Lisa had made it dirty. It is ready for you to put on to-night. You can go and dress in Jimmy's caravan, Mrs. Brown says, and she will see that your dress is all right. Now dry your eyes and be cheerful, for goodness' sake!"

Mrs. Brown had ironed Lotta's pretty, shining frock, and it looked beautiful. It was on a hanger at the end of Mrs. Brown's spotless caravan, waiting for Lotta to put on that evening.

"Lotta will love riding Black Beauty in the ring again,"

thought Mrs. Brown. "It's a pity that the child has had such a bad time lately—but I really think she is nicer now, so perhaps she has learnt a few lessons. How I shall miss her when we leave!"

Jimmy was helping Laddo with the dogs. Lal was with her beloved horses. Mrs. Brown looked at the clock and hoped that Lotta wouldn't come in too late to change. "I want to give her hair a good brush, and see that she gets a really good wash," said Mrs. Brown. "She doesn't look as if she has washed properly for days, the little monkey!"

The hands of the clock moved on slowly. Lotta was late! Mrs. Brown looked out of her caravan to find the little girl.

"Lotta!" she called. "Lotta! Hurry up! It's getting late!"

But Lotta didn't answer. She wasn't anywhere nearby, so Mrs. Brown hurried over to Jimmy.

"Jimmy! For goodness' sake find Lotta and tell her she really must come now. I want to get her clean and tidy, and see that her frock is all right. Hurry now—she must be somewhere over at the other end of the field."

"Right, Mother," said Jimmy, who had nearly finished his job. He put down the last dish of fresh water in the dogs' big cage and ran off to get Lotta.

"I guess she's hiding away so that she doesn't have to go into the ring with Lisa and Jeanne," thought the boy, who understood fierce little Lotta very well indeed. "I don't blame her! I'd just hate to share my turn with those horrid girls."

He called Lotta. There was no answer. He looked under all the caravans, but no Lotta was there. He even stood on tiptoe and looked on top of the vans, for since Lisa and Jeanne had come, Lotta had often climbed to the roofs with the two girls.

At last Jimmy gave it up. He went back to his caravan, and called to his mother.

"Mother! I can't find Lotta. I'm afraid she's hiding. I've looked everywhere."

"The naughty little girl!" said Mrs. Brown, vexed. "Really, she thinks she can do exactly as she likes! Here

I've got everything ready for her—and she'll be very late."

"Mother, I don't think Lotta means to go into the ring with Lisa and Jeanne," said Jimmy. "I think she's hidden herself away so that she shan't."

"Well, she will get into serious trouble with Britomart then," said Mrs. Brown anxiously. "Look—here are Lisa and Jeanne—perhaps they know where Lotta is."

But they didn't. They were surprised to hear that Lotta was not to be found. Lisa nudged Jeanne with her elbow and whispered something to her. Jimmy couldn't hear what it was.

The two girls ran off to Britomart's caravan. Jimmy watched them. "Nasty tell-tales!" he said. "Look, Mother —they've gone to tell Britomart that Lotta's hiding. How they do love to get people into trouble!"

But they had gone to say something else as well! Lisa knocked on Britomart's door, and he called out in his deep voice, "Come in!"

Lisa opened the door timidly. Britomart glared at her. "Oh—it's you. Have you got a message from your father?"

"No, Mr. Britomart," said Lisa. "We've just come to say that Lotta won't go into the ring with us to-night. She's hiding!"

"I will not have such disobedience!" Britomart growled. "Her father shall whip her for this."

"I know how you could punish her," said Lisa boldly. "She loves her pony, Black Beauty, and she won't let any-one else ride him. But *I* could ride him, Mr. Britomart! And when Lotta hears that some one else has taken her own pony into the ring, she will be sorry that she disobeyed you."

Britomart looked at the red-haired Lisa and her sly little face. "Very well," he said shortly. "Get her pony and ride it. It will teach her to come to her senses."

Lisa and Jeanne flew off, afraid that Britomart would change his mind. To ride Black Beauty in the ring! This was something that the little girls had always longed to do.

They ran to tell Jimmy. He was astonished to see them running back so quickly, looking so excited.

"Jimmy! Get Black Beauty out for us! Britomart says we can ride him in the ring to-night, as Lotta won't."

"You horrid little tell-tales," said Jimmy. "No—I won't get Black Beauty for you! Get him yourself—and I hope he bites you!"

Jimmy slammed the caravan door in a rage. Lisa and Jeanne rushed off to the stables, pretty little figures in their bunchy dresses sewn with glittering sequins. Nobody would have guessed that they could be such horrid little girls.

They flung open the door of the stable-van and went to Black Beauty's stall.

It was empty! No Black Beauty was there! "Where is he?" said Lisa in dismay. "He must be in one of the other stalls."

The two girls hurriedly ran down the stable-vans and looked for Black Beauty. But only the other circus-horses were there, sleek and satiny, looking in surprise at the two excited children.

"He's *not* here," said Jeanne. "Then where is he?"

"With Lotta, of course," said Lisa angrily.

"But where's Lotta?" said Jeanne.

"Goodness knows!" said Lisa. "Not hiding in the camp, anyway. *She* could hide herself, but she couldn't hide a big creature like Black Beauty. She's gone off somewhere on him. Goodness—Britomart will be angry, won't he? He forbade Lotta to ride the pony by herself out of the camp."

The girls rushed to tell every one. Jimmy was worried at once, and so were Lal and Mrs. Brown. Lotta was such a monkey—goodness knows where she would go or when she would come back! And what would happen to her when she did come back? Some horrid punishment again, Jimmy was sure.

"She'll come back to-night, after the show," said Mrs. Brown, comforting him. "Don't worry, Jimmy. She's just taken Black Beauty away so that Lisa and Jeanne can't ride him in the ring. I expect she guessed that they might try to."

"Yes—that's it," said Jimmy, feeling better. He had not forgotten how once before Lotta had run away, dressed as a boy—and he didn't want to think she might have done that again. So he hoped and hoped that Lotta would be in the field waiting for him when the show was over that evening.

But Lotta wasn't. She didn't come back at all that night. Every one was cross and worried about it. What would the mad little girl do next? It was really too bad to behave like that.

"She's taken her new doll with her," said Lal, appearing at the door of her caravan. "Now why did she do that? Oh dear, wherever is the child?"

And where *was* Lotta? Why had she gone, and what was she doing? Ah, she had made her own plans—and very strange plans they were, too!

LOTTA'S BIG ADVENTURE

LOTTA had been very upset and angry to think that she must stay behind with Lal and Laddo, and work under Britomart for at least half a year more.

"Jimmy will be gone, and little dog Lucky—and kind Mrs. Brown—and Mr. Wally and Sammy—and Mr. Volla and the bears—and dear old Tonky and Jumbo—and Oona. Oh, I can't bear it!"

The little girl was lying under her caravan with Lulu the old spaniel, who licked her every now and again, sad that Lotta was unhappy. Lotta took a stick and dug it into the ground. She drew some letters—and they were the ones that little dog Lucky used to spell out so cleverly every day—G-A-L-L-I-A-N-O.

"Oh, Mr. Galliano, if only you knew what is happening to your famous circus, you would try to come back quickly!" said Lotta. "You'd stick your top-hat straight up on your head, look fierce, and tell Britomart he's no good. Oh, if only you would come back!"

Lotta dug her stick hard into the ground, wishing that she was sticking it into Britomart! Then a thought came into her head.

"I wonder what Mr. Galliano would do if he heard that we are most of us going to leave his circus," she said to herself. "I wonder if anyone has told him. I know Britomart wouldn't, because he would be sure that Galliano would be angry and disappointed. I guess he's only told him the good things and not the bad."

Lotta began to think about going into the ring that night with Lisa and Jeanne. She was quite determined not to— but she knew that Britomart would be very angry indeed if she disobeyed again. "I think I shall take Black Beauty

143

and ride away until the show is over to-night," thought the little girl. "If I say I won't go into the ring, Britomart is quite horrid enough to say that those two red-haired creatures can have my pony to ride. And I won't have that! I'll ride away, far away—and perhaps I shall come to where Galliano is with Mrs. Galliano."

Now no sooner had she said that to herself than Lotta sat up straight in excitement, banging her head hard against the underneath of the caravan. But she didn't even feel the bump.

"Gracious! Why didn't I think of that before! I'll *go* to Galliano and tell him all that's happened—and maybe he will turn Britomart out of the circus and put Mr. Wally or somebody in his place. Oh, goody, goody! That *is* an idea!"

Lotta was so excited that Lulu became excited too and barked.

"Sh!" said Lotta. "I don't want anyone to know where I am. We'll wait here till there's not many people about, Lulu, and then I'll slip out and get Black Beauty—and darling Rosemary, of course. I shan't leave *her* behind for Lisa to get."

Lotta wondered where Mr. Galliano was staying. She knew that Mrs. Galliano was out of hospital now, and that they were both staying somewhere whilst Mrs. Galliano got better. How could she find out? She did not dare to ask Britomart, and she was sure that no one else knew, for the circus-folk rarely wrote letters. Some of them could not even read or write.

"I'll get into Britomart's caravan and find the letter from Mr. Galliano," thought Lolla. "I hope he doesn't carry it about in his pocket. Lulu, we can see Britomart's caravan from here. We'll watch and see if he goes out."

Britomart did go out, and it wasn't long before Lotta was creeping out from under her caravan. No one was about except Mr. Tonks, and he was rubbing Jumbo with oil, and paid no attention to Lotta. The little girl ran quickly over to Britomart's caravan. She was up the steps in a trice, and shut the door. She looked around. Where would Britomart keep his letters?

It was easy to see. There was a small desk at the back of the caravan—and on it were spread a few letters and bills. In a trice Lotta spied Galliano's last letter, slipped it down the front of her frock, and ran from the caravan. Nobody saw her. Nobody knew what she had done. Lotta squeezed under her caravan again and looked at the letter. How glad she was that she had taken lessons from kind Mrs. Brown and knew how to read.

She read the address at the top of the letter: "British Hotel, Langley Holme, Devon." Lotta had no idea where Devon was, but she didn't care. She could always ask. She stuffed the letter back and slipped out again. This time she found a small bag and put into it some bread, some cheese, biscuits, chocolate—and her doll! That was all.

Then she watched to see when she could get Black Beauty out without being seen. She had a very good chance, quite unexpectedly. Two of the zebras, who were being exercised at the other end of the field, were suddenly frightened by a cow that poked its head over the hedge. One escaped from Zeno, and he yelled for help, for a frightened zebra is dangerous.

Every one ran to catch the zebra, or to see what was happening. Jimmy went too—and so Lotta could not tell him what she was going to do.

She was sorry about that. She did not want to slip away without seeing Jimmy—and besides, she thought he could tell Lal and Laddo of her plans. She dared not tell her father and mother herself, in case they forbade her to go, and fierce little Lotta was quite determined to do what she had made up her mind to do.

She got Black Beauty out easily. She slipped on to his back, whispered into his ear, and cantered quickly to the nearest hedge. She did not dare to go out of the big field-gate, for she was certain to be seen if she did. So she set Black Beauty at the high hedge, and the horse rose beautifully into the air, cleared the hedge, and galloped over the next field. Lotta was safe!

Lotta rode on all that afternoon. She had stopped a party of school-children and asked them which was the way to Devon. They stared at the bright-eyed little girl on her beautiful horse, and thought she was marvellous. One boy got out his school atlas from his bag.

"Look," he said, "I'll show you exactly where you are now, and you will see that Devon is the next county to this. This is Dorset."

He opened the atlas, and showed her the map of England. Lotta had learnt just a little geography from Mrs. Brown, and she looked closely at the map.

"What a lucky thing for me that Devon is the next county, and not somewhere right at the top of the map," she said. "Does your map show a place called Langley Holme, boy?"

"No," said the boy, looking at it. "It doesn't. Whereabouts is it?"

"I wouldn't be asking you if I knew," said Lotta. "Oh dear—how am I to know if Langley Holme is at the top of Devon or at the bottom."

"It's on the south coast, near a big port called Plymouth," said a little girl shyly. "My auntie used to live there. That's how I know. Show her Plymouth on the map, John."

Plymouth was easy to see. "That's good," said Lotta, pleased. "It's on the sea-coast, isn't it? I must just look out for sign-posts marked Plymouth, and go steadily on till I get there. Then I can ask for Langley Holme."

She galloped off, and the school-children looked after her admiringly.

Lotta rode on steadily, delighted to see "Plymouth" on a sign-post at the next cross-roads. She made up her mind to give Black Beauty a good long rest about seven o'clock, and a feed and water, and then to ride on all the night. "Then if people start looking for me, trying to get me back before I've seen Mr. Galliano, they won't be able to—because I'll have nearly got there to-morrow," she said to her doll Rosemary, who was sitting just in front of Lotta, smiling away as if she was really enjoying her strange ride.

At seven o'clock Lotta and Black Beauty took their rest. Black Beauty was a strong horse and was not at all tired. He was longing to gallop on and on with his little mistress sitting sturdily on his back. He could not understand why

146

Lotta and he were going so far, but he didn't care. He would take Lotta to the end of the world if she wanted him to!

At nine o'clock they were off again, the doll sitting in front of Lotta once more. The moon rose after a while, and it was easy for Lotta to read the sign-posts. Many people stared in wonder at the curly-haired girl riding on so steadily, but she was gone before they could even shout to ask her where she was going.

All night the little girl rode on. When dawn came she was so tired that she could no longer sit on Black Beauty's back. She saw an old rick standing in a field and slipped off her horse. She gave him a drink and a rub, and then told him to eat the grass. She cuddled up against the rick, shut her eyes, and at once fell fast asleep.

Nobody saw her there, and nobody saw Black Beauty, who soon came to lie down near his sleeping mistress. It was noon when Lotta awoke and stretched herself. She remembered where she was, and leapt to her feet. She rinsed her face in a little stream and shook back her curls. She finished up all the food she had brought with her, and leapt on to Black Beauty's back again. The horse whinnied with joy. So he and Lotta were to go galloping on once more!

Plymouth was farther than Lotta thought, but gradually the miles shown on each sign-post grew less and less—and at last, towards evening, another name appeared on a sign-post. Lotta squealed with joy.

"Langley Holme, two miles. Oh, Black Beauty, we are nearly there! We don't even have to go to Plymouth. It's before we come to Plymouth. Come on—we'll soon see dear old Mr. Galliano and Mrs. Galliano too! You've never seen them, Rosemary—but you'll love them."

She galloped on, very tired now, but much happier; and soon she came to a quiet little seaside place, with a pretty sandy beach where people bathed. On a little hill nearby stood a big hotel, with golden letters across it: "British Hotel."

"Just the place we're looking for," said Lotta happily. She rode down the street that led to the sea, turned up along the promenade, and went on towards the big hotel. A great many people sat on a verandah outside, drinking, and eating ices. How they stared when the dirty, untidy little girl rode up, her horse's hooves sounding loudly in the street!

Lotta gazed along the row of surprised people, looking for Mr. Galliano. Every one stared at her. Whatever did this strange little girl want? What was she doing here, stopping outside the hotel, staring at every one? The hall-porter came out and spoke sharply to her.

"Go away! Don't stare like that, little girl."

"Is Mr. Galliano here?" asked Lotta. "I want Mr. Galliano."

"I certainly shan't tell any of our guests that *you* want him," said the rude porter. "Now, go away. "

Lotta stared at him, her lips beginning to tremble, for she was very tired and anxious. And then, just as she was turning Black Beauty round, she heard an enormous shout.

"LOTTA! MY LITTLE LOTTA! What are you doing here?" And out of the hotel rushed dear old Galliano, his eyes nearly falling out of his head in surprise!

LOTTA GETS HER WAY

LOTTA gave a squeal of joy. Yes—it was Mr. Galliano, though he looked quite different, dressed in white flannels and a shirt, instead of in his usual riding-breeches, top-boots, and top-hat. He was fatter, too, but his jolly face was just the same, and his moustaches stuck up stiffly as they always did.

"LOTTA!" he yelled. "Is it really Lotta?"

"Yes," said Lotta, and she slipped down from Black Beauty. She was so tired that her legs would not stand under her. Mr. Galliano picked her up in his arms, nodded to the porter to take Black Beauty, and carried the little girl into the hotel. Every one stared in amazement, but neither Lotta nor Galliano cared. Let them stare!

Galliano took Lotta into his own sitting-room, and there sat Mrs. Galliano, much thinner and paler, but with her same gentle smile. How amazed she was to see Lotta in Galliano's arms!

"Lotta!" she cried. "How did you come here? Is any-one with you?"

"Only Black Beauty and Rosemary," said Lotta, setting her doll down beside Mrs. Galliano. She looked happily round, and settled herself comfortably on Galliano's knee. She flung her arms around his neck and hugged him. She took Mrs. Galliano's hand and squeezed it. Tears came into her eyes and fell down her cheeks, but she smiled all the time because she was so happy to be with the Gallianos once more.

Mrs. Galliano pressed a bell nearby, and ordered hot milk and biscuits for Lotta from the waiter. "Eat and drink before you tell your story," she said. "There is plenty of time."

So Lotta ate and drank—but she told her story at once, with her mouth full, for she could not wait.

"Oh, Mr. Galliano, your circus is all breaking up," she said. "Mr. Wally's going, and Mr. Volla, and Tonky, and Oona, and Jimmy, and——"

"But why?" cried Galliano in astonishment. "Nobody told me this. Each time I hear from Britomart he tells me how marvellous the show has been going, and what a lot of money comes in, yes! What is the matter then?"

"Oh, the show has gone well," said Lotta, "but, Mr. Galliano, we do hate Britomart so. Do you know that he has never once smiled since you left? "

"Well, I can't see that that matters much," said Galliano, puzzled. "Something more must have happened besides that, yes!"

So Lotta told him how stern Britomart had been, how he had forbidden Jimmy to play with the animals, how Sammy was moping, how Mr. Wally had quarrelled with the ringmaster, and how she, Lotta, had been, forbidden to go into the ring for something that was not her fault.

"And oh, Mr. Galliano, every one is so angry and miserable, and nobody will stay with Britomart—except Lal and Laddo, who signed a paper to say they would stay with the circus for a year. And that means I have to stay too. And I just couldn't stay without Jimmy and Lucky, so I came to find you and tell you. Mr. Galliano, dear Mr. Galliano, can't you do something?"

Then Mrs. Galliano spoke in her slow, soft voice. "My little Lotta, there is only one thing for Galliano to do. He must go back. He cannot see his famous circus split up so that there is nothing for him to return to when I am better."

"But, Tessa, you are not better yet—and I promised you that I would stay until you too were well enough to come back to the circus, yes!" said Mr. Galliano, rubbing his right ear in a very worried manner. "I cannot break my promise, no."

"You want to make me happy, Galliano, don't you?" went on Mrs. Galliano. "Well, I shall only be happy if you go back and become ring-master again in your own circus.

I will not go to the South of France. I will stay here in this peaceful place, where I have my friends around me. And in six months' time I too will come back. I am so much better already! If you stay here with me, and let your circus go to pieces, I shall be so sad that I shall fall ill again. And you would not like that, Galliano."

"No—no, indeed, I should not like that," said the ring-master, gazing at his wife anxiously. "Well, Tessa, you are always right, yes. I know that. Never have you given me bad advice, no, never. So I will go back to Galliano's Circus, and it shall be mine once more! And Britomart must go!"

Lotta gave such a squeal that Mrs. Galliano jumped. The little girl flung herself on Mrs. Galliano and pressed her cheek to hers. "Oh, Mrs. Galliano, you dear, kind, unselfish person! Can you really spare Mr. Galliano to come back to us? We do want him so much. Oh, how glad I am I came and told you everything!"

"Now, now, you must leave me some breath, child!" said Mrs. Galliano, laughing. "Yes, of course Galliano must go back. Why, if he does not return soon to his circus, he will be so fat with sitting about that he will not be able to get into his riding-breeches and coat any more! A fat ring-master is a poor sight."

Lotta was so excited and glad that she could not keep still. "I want to ride straight back and tell the others," she cried. "Where's Black Beauty? I'll start now and tell every one else. Oh, how glad they will be!"

"No, no, Lotta, you can't do that," said Mrs. Galliano. "You are tired out. You must stay here for the night. You will like to see this hotel. It has a fine big bath with taps that run hot and cold water, and a towel-rail that keeps your towels warm and dry. And——"

But Lotta would not listen. "I'm not tired," she cried, "I'm not, I'm not! Oh, do let me get Black Beauty and go back again! I know the way."

"My dear child, even if you are not tired out, Black Beauty is," said Galliano. "You don't want to ruin him by over-riding, do you? He will be no use if you do."

"Oh no, I don't!" said Lotta at once. "Yes—he must

be tired, the darling. I'll go and see to him. Come on, Rosemary."

"No, Lotta," said Mrs. Galliano. "There are men to see to Black Beauty, and he will be quite happy. You are to come to my room and go to bed. I will have a little bed put by our big one, and you will love to sleep there."

Lotta really was so tired that she could hardly walk to the big bedroom, whose windows looked out over the calm blue sea. She had a bath in a marvellous green bath, and dried herself with a big soft towel from the hot towel-rail. Then she ate some ice-cream pudding, curled up in the dear little bed beside Mrs. Galliano's, and fell fast asleep in a trice. The doll lay beside her, its long-lashed eyes closed, just like Lotta's.

The two Gallianos looked down on the little girl, and then looked across at one another. "She is a wild little thing," said Mrs. Galliano, "but how full of courage she is! It is good that she came to tell you all that has happened, Galliano. You have been fretting for your circus, I know—and now it is clear that you must go back."

Mr. Galliano sent a telegram to Lal to say that Lotta was safe with them. Lal could not believe her eyes when she read that Lotta was in Langley Holme with the Gallianos!

"But how did she get there—how did she know the way —why did she run away to them—how did she know where they were?" she kept saying to every one a hundred times. But nobody knew the answers. Only Jimmy smiled a little secret smile to himself.

"Lotta could do anything in the world if she once made up her mind to do it," he thought proudly. "There's no stopping that little monkey if she means to do something. I'm often cross with her, and would like to shake her, but she's a dear, brave girl and I'm proud of her. I know why she went to the Gallianos—to tell them about Britomart. I wonder if they'll be able to do anything. My word—Britomart looks as black as thunder now he knows where Lotta is!"

And Britomart certainly did look black. His great eye-

would have kept these folk happy, yes—but all you gave them was harsh words and punishments."

"Galliano, you have spoilt the people in this circus," said Britomart in his usual cold, deep voice, his black eyes flashing. "They are disobedient, rude, and quarrelsome. No man can manage a camp like this."

"I have managed it for years," said Galliano, "and I am going to manage it again, yes."

"Every one is leaving— except Zeno, some of the clowns, and Pierre," said Britomart.

"No one is leaving—except those you say!" said Mr. Galliano, putting his hat on straight and looking stern. "Britomart, take your share of the money and what performers will go with you. Make your own circus, if you can—you will not keep it long until you learn that only one thing rules a camp, and that is kindness, yes!"

Mr. Galliano left the caravan, his hat still straight on his head. Britomart was left alone. He stared after the old ring-master, and a sad look came into his big black eyes. He knew himself to be a cleverer man than Galliano— but he was impatient and scornful where Mr. Galliano was kind and understanding. He was a lonely and unhappy man—but it was his own fault.

"If I get another chance, I'll try Galliano's ideas," he thought. "Look at the circus-folk out there, crowding round him—they never gave me those smiles and handshakes and claps on the back. They'll all stay with him—and I shall be left with Pierre and one or two others. I shan't try to make a new circus—I shall go off again on my own, and be Britomart the conjurer."

So that evening Britomart packed his things, cleared Galliano's caravan for him, and drove off in his magnificent blue-and-silver car. He said good-bye to no one, for he was a disappointed and rather ashamed man. No one waved to him. No one wished him luck. He was gone, and nobody cared. Poor Britomart—the worst enemy he had was himself.

What an evening that was in the camp! It happened to be the last evening of the show, and Galliano, of course, was to be ring-master.

"We'll make it the best show we've ever given," cried Sticky Stanley in delight, turning six somersaults at once. "And, Lotta, you'll be able to have your turn again!"

Galliano forbade Lisa and Jeanne to go into the ring —much to Jimmy's delight and Lotta's. Now that he knew how those two unpleasant children had got Jimmy and Lotta into trouble, Galliano had no time for them, and ordered them out of his way whenever they came near to beg him to let them go into the ring that last splendid evening.

"You have a lesson to learn, yes!" he shouted at red-haired Lisa. "I will treat you as Britomart treated Lotta— you will both go to your caravan and STAY THERE! And if I see you out of it, I will chase you with my big whip, yes."

Of course every one knew that Galliano would do nothing of the sort, but Lisa and Jeanne were very much afraid he might. So they scuttled off to their caravan, crying bitterly, and Lotta and Jimmy watched them go.

"Well, it isn't kind to be glad when people are unhappy," said Jimmy, "but really, Lotta, those two deserve a bit of trouble now."

"I hope they get lots," said Lotta fiercely. Then she laughed. "Oh, Jimmy—I'm so happy now, that I can't even feel really fierce about Lisa and Jeanne! I just don't care about them any more. In fact, I'm so happy that I might even go and show them my lovely new doll! They've never seen her yet."

"Don't you do anything of the sort," said Jimmy. "Why, you might find yourself feeling so happy you'd *give* Rosemary to Lisa!"

"Oh!" said Lotta with a squeal. "You know I'd never do that. Come on, Jimmy—it's time we got ready for the show. We shall do our turn together again. I shall ride dear old Black Beauty in the ring, and hear the claps and shouts. And it will be Mr. Galliano standing in the middle, cracking his whip, instead of stern old Britomart!"

Lotta danced off to put on her sparkling circus-frock. The little girl was so happy that her eyes shone like stars. It was Galliano's Circus again—Jimmy was staying on with Lucky—things would be the same as they used to be. And it was she, Lotta, who had found Mr. Galliano and got him back! No wonder Lotta felt proud and excited and happy.

An hour before the circus began, a caravan came up the lane to the field. It was bright orange with blue wheels —and Jimmy knew it at once.

"Lotta! Lotta! Quick! Here's Madame Prunella come back again—hark at her parrots all screeching!"

And sure enough it was! Somehow Prunella had heard the news that Britomart was gone and Galliano was back, and she too had come to join in the last night of the show. Oh, what fun! How the plump little woman hugged and kissed every one, and how the parrots screeched and squealed!

"Fried fish and chips, fried fish and chips!" yelled Gringle in excitement, and the children laughed in delight.

"Good old Gringle! We *have* missed you!"

It was a splendid show that night, for every one was happy and determined to do their best for Galliano. He stood in the middle of the ring, his hat well on one side, his sunburnt face very happy indeed. The only things that made him feel uncomfortable were his clothes! They really were much too tight for him now.

The people clapped and shouted and cheered till they were hoarse. They stamped their feet at the end of the show, and waved their hats and handkerchiefs.

"Best circus we've ever seen!" they said to one another. "Quite the best!"

It was late before every one went to bed that night. How they talked! How they sang and laughed in the camp, till the dogs got restless and whined, and Lucky fell fast asleep in her master's arms.

Galliano sent them all off to their caravans at last. They stumbled up the steps, yawning, but very happy. The circus was not to split up after all! They were all to go on the road as usual.

All? Well, not quite all. Google did not want to stay, for he said there were too many children in the camp for his liking. And Pierre was not going with the circus either, for Galliano had heard from Mrs. Brown that Lisa and Jeanne would be better away. Also Pierre had been friendly with Britomart, so that no one really felt that they wanted him to stay.

Jimmy was sorry that Neptune was to go, for he liked the clever seal. But never mind, Madame Prunella was back again with her flock of wonderful parrots. Zeno was staying, and Twinkle and Pippi, so the circus was very big still, and had plenty of performers.

"Good-night, Jimmy," said Lotta, going to her own caravan. "Isn't everything lovely now?"

"Yes—and all because you were such a fierce little girl and wouldn't put up with the horrid things that were happening," said Jimmy. "Good for you, Lotta! I'm proud of you!"

The two children were soon fast asleep. Lulu the spaniel lay on Lotta's feet, and Rosemary the doll was beside her. Little dog Lucky was on Jimmy's toes, and they all dreamed happily of the good days to come."

"Good old Galliano!" said Jimmy in his sleep. "I'm so glad you're back again, Galliano—good old Galliano!"